Jessica Sorensen lives in Wyoming with her husband and three children. She is the author of numerous romance novels. All of her New Adult novels have been *New York Times* and ebook bestsellers.

Keep in contact with Jessica:

jessicasorensensblog.blogspot.co.uk
Facebook/Jessica Sorensen
@jessFallenStar

Praise for Jessica Sorensen

The Destiny of Violet & Luke

'Gripping and heartbreaking . . . You will be hooked, and you won't be able to not come back'
ReviewingRomance.com

'Sorensen's intense and realistic stories never cease to amaze me and entice my interest. She is an incredible writer as she captures the raw imperfections of the beautiful and the damned'
TheCelebrityCafe.com

The Redemption of Callie & Kayden

'I couldn't put it down. This was just as dark, beautiful, and compelling as the first [book] . . . Nothing short of amazing . . . Never have I read such emotional characters where everything that has happened to them seems so real'
OhMyShelves.com

'A love story that will overflow your heart with hope. This series is not to be missed'
UndertheCoversBookblog.com

Breaking Nova

'*Breaking Nova* is one of those books that just sticks with you. I was thinking about it when I wasn't reading it, wondering what was going to happen with Nova . . . an all-consuming, heartbreaking story'
BooksLiveForever.com

'Heartbreaking, soul-shattering, touching, and unforgettable . . . Jessica Sorenson is an amazingly talented author'
ABookishEscape.com

The Temptation of Lila & Ethan

'Sorensen has true talent to capture your attention with each word written. She is creatively talented . . . Through the mist of demons that consume the characters' souls she manages to find beauty in their broken lives'
TheCelebrityCafe.com

'An emotional, romantic, and really great contemporary romance . . . Lila and Ethan's story is emotionally raw, devastating, and heart-wrenching'
AlwaysYAatHeart.com

The Resolution of Callie & Kayden

JESSICA SORENSEN

sphere

SPHERE

First published in Great Britain in 2015 by Sphere

1 3 5 7 9 10 8 6 4 2

A CIP catalogue record for this book is available from the British Library.

ISBN 978-0-7515-5884-5

Typeset in Adobe Garamond by Palimpsest Book Production Limited,
Falkirk, Stirlingshire
Printed and bound in Great Britain by Clays Ltd, St Ives plc

Papers used by Sphere are from well-managed forests
and other responsible sources.

MIX
Paper from
responsible sources
FSC
www.fsc.org
FSC® C104740

Sphere
An imprint of
Little, Brown Book Group
Carmelite House
50 Victoria Embankment
London EC4Y 0DZ

An Hachette UK Company
www.hachette.co.uk

www.littlebrown.co.uk

The Resolution of Callie & Kayden

Prologue

#103 Outrun Your Demons.

Kayden

Run.

Throw.

Catch.

Duck.

Run.

Run.

Run.

My father's words scream from behind me like a ghost as I race around the track. I can't outrun them, escape them, hide from them. My feet pound against the dirt as my lungs tighten in my chest, my entire body dripping with sweat even though it's barely fifty degrees and I'm wearing shorts. My pulse is pounding, my limbs aching, begging me to stop. That it's enough.

But nothing ever feels like enough.

I can't outrun him.

His voice.

His words he drilled in me.

I want to be free from it. Free from him. My mom. My past. The years of abuse. What I want is my resolution. But to get it, I need to let go and I can't let go when everything is so unknown.

I don't know where he is – what he's doing. If he's alive. Dead. If he's sorry for what he did. And I might never know. Just like I might never be able to let go.

So all I can do is *run*.

Until I can no longer breathe.

Until my limbs can no longer move.

Until my heart stops beating.

Until maybe his voice will disappear.

Chapter 1

#101 Jump on the Bed. A Lot.

Callie

Wintertime is beautiful. Snowflakes tumbling from the sky and swirling through the air. They remind me that the world is always changing, that people are always changing, that I'm always changing. This reminder is what keeps me happy, moving forward in my life, letting go of what happened with Caleb, and living my life for the future. A future that is filled with endless possibilities.

Despite my positivity, I do feel like something has been missing from my life lately, but I can't figure out what it is exactly. It's not necessarily a bad thing. In fact, it might be good. Like sadness and pain perhaps. Or possibly that I'm moving more freely through life than I ever have. Or perhaps I'm just looking for something to explain this strange, new, liberating feeling residing in my heart, because the past seems so distant now. The person who hurt me has vanished and even though there was no resolution for what he did to me, I feel like my inner demons connected to him – what he did – have been resolved. Yes, the memories are still there, scarring my past, but they don't define me anymore.

And I feel . . . well, happy.

I want us to share with Kayden, because he seems a little sad lately. Not like how he was before, though. No, he's much better than he was a year ago when I met him in the clinic that horrible day, the place where he was sent because nurses and doctors thought he'd stabbed himself. While he had self-harmed, his father was the one who made the start and the worst of the injuries that had nearly killed him and almost ruined the future we have now.

The beautiful one that we have now.

'Knock, knock, knock.' Seth raps on the door as he cracks it open and sticks his head in. 'Hey, what's up with you not answering your texts?'

I set the pen down in the spine of my journal and pick up my phone from off the bed. 'Sorry, I forgot I turned it down for class.' I press the volume up while he fakes a pout and enters my dorm room.

He looks all kinds of Seth stylish in his black and grey sweater, dark blue jeans, and Converse sneakers, his honey-blond highlighted hair tousled to perfection.

'Hot date tonight?' I ask as I set my phone down on the nightstand and shut my journal.

'Whatever do you mean?' He taps his finger on his lips, feigning ignorance, like he hasn't been chattering about his date with Greyson all week, the date that marks the first anniversary of when they officially considered themselves dating.

I tuck my journal underneath my pillow and get off the bed and to my feet, smoothing out the creases in my violet and black striped shirt. 'I mean, the date you've been yammering about for weeks now. *The* date. The one that marks your first anniversary.'

He kicks the door shut. 'You need to stop paying so much attention to me. It ruins all my fun and mysteriousness.'

'You're never mysterious,' I say, putting my long brown hair up in a ponytail. 'But we can do a redo if you want to? You can go back out and enter again, and I can pretend that I have no idea why you're dressed up. Then you can announce the news to me and we can celebrate and jump up and down and scream, "Oh my God!"' I wave my hands in front of

5

me while I bounce up and down. "It's going to be so epically awesome!"

He stares at me for a moment, pretending not to be amused, but then the corners of his mouth turn upward and he starts jumping up and down with me. 'Let's just skip to the good part,' he says, laughing as he leaps onto my bed and bounces on the mattress, offering his hand to help me up.

'Why, thank you, sir.' I grab his hand and he pulls me up with him.

We continue to jump on the bed like kids, yelling about his anniversary until my roommate, Harper, walks into the room. She stops dead in her tracks at the sight of us, standing on the bed, red-faced and panting with our hands in the air.

'Hey, Harper.' I wave at her as I stop jumping on the mattress. Seth continues, though, unbothered that he looks like a complete lunatic, but he also doesn't have to share a room with her the entire year either.

Harper gives an intrigued glance at Seth and me as she steps into the room and closes the door behind her. 'What are you guys doing?'

Seth begins to bounce exaggeratedly on the bed. 'Exercising,' he jokes, breathless.

'Great idea. I'll have to try it sometime. Although

I'm a two-person kind of jumping-on-the-bed girl myself.' Harper winks, but something about it looks wrong, like she's just playing a part in the moment, being how she thinks she needs to be. She's that way a lot. Then she walks over to the desk near the window to set her books down.

Seth giggles at her remark, while I feel a blush rush to my cheeks. Even now, after having sex, I still get embarrassed over sexual innuendos. I used to think it was because I was raped when I was twelve by my brother's then best friend, and it had left that kind of a mark on me, but now I'm coming to realize that it might just be my personality.

'So, what are you two up to for the day?' Harper asks as she pulls her long blonde hair up in a messy bun before picking up her iPod from off her bed.

Seth shrugs as he hops off the bed and lands on the floor with a thud. 'Not anything right now. Why? You looking for a party buddy again?'

She wavers, slightly distracted as she shuffles through the list of songs on her iPod. 'I was thinking about going to this frat party tonight, but I'm still on the fence.'

Seth makes a gagging face as he mock-clutches his neck. 'Frat boys. Yuck.'

7

'For sure,' she agrees, reaching for her headphones on her pillow. 'But I need to get out of this tiny box of a room for a night or I'm going to go crazy.'

'Well, sorry, but you're going to have to ride solo on this one,' Seth tells her. The two of them occasionally see each other at parties and hang out, but that's about as far as their friendship extends.

'Bummer.' She smiles at me, but it doesn't reach her eyes. 'What about you, Callie? You down for a party?'

'I'm with Seth on this one,' I reply, feeling kind of guilty when she frowns. 'I'm not into frat parties.'

She shrugs it off, seeming a little depressed. But once she notices me noticing her plummeting cheeriness, she forces a bright smile, then puts her earbuds in. I'm not sure why, but Harper seems lonely all the time, even though she's always surrounded by people. She keeps smiling as she moves for her bed, but I've given enough fake smiles in my life to recognize one when I see it.

As she flops down and gets situated to do her homework, Seth waves at her then takes me by the elbow and pulls me toward the door. 'Let's go get some coffee,' he says, grabbing my hoodie from the bedpost and shoving it at me, 'and I'll tell you about the present I got Greyson.'

Slipping on my jacket, I follow Seth out the door and head down the hallway to the elevators.

'So it's a collection of things we've done together,' he says as I push the bottom floor. 'Like movies we've watched, music we've listened to and food we both agree are awesome.'

'That might be the coolest present ever,' I tell him as we reach the bottom floor and step out into the lounge area.

'I know, right?' he says as we stroll toward the door. It's a breezy yet beautiful day to be walking beneath the crystal blue sky. Frost clings to the branches of the leafless trees that surround the building and the frozen grass makes the entire scene look like a winter wonderland.

'So what's new with you?' Seth asks as we steer in the direction of the nearest coffee house, which is kitty corner to the University of Wyoming – the college we both attend. 'It feels like ages since I've talked to you.'

I laugh because it's only been like a day. 'Not much.'

'How's the new job coming?'

I sigh. I got an internship writing for an online newspaper at the beginning of the semester. I love writing and everything but . . . 'It's kind of not what

I was expecting,' I tell him as we step off the grass and onto the slippery sidewalk.

'What do you mean?' he asks as we link arms before one of us wipes out.

I give a half shrug. 'I just wish I could write . . . I don't know, whatever I want, instead of certain things. It feels like such a job.' I sigh. 'That makes me sound selfish, doesn't it? And ungrateful.'

Seth chuckles as he maneuvers us around a large ice patch in the center of the sidewalk. 'No, it makes you sound normal. You don't have to like a job just because it's your job.'

I tuck my free hand into the pocket of my jacket as the wind bites at my skin. 'Yeah, I guess you're right.'

'No, not guess I'm right; I *am* right.' He shoots me a conceited grin. 'I'm always right when it comes to advice.' He gets a thoughtful look on his face. 'And speaking of advice, why haven't you talked to Kayden about moving in together? I thought we talked about that a couple of weeks ago and you were going to finally' – he makes an air quote with his free hand – '"Go for it."'

I cringe internally at the painful reminder. 'I already told you I decided not to.'

'I know, but I was hoping you changed your mind. I think you're wrong about Kayden not being ready for that big of a step. And even if he isn't ready, I still think you should know where he stands,' he tells me as we halt at the corner of the sidewalk, waiting to cross the street. 'You guys have been together way longer than Greyson and me, or Luke and Violet.'

'Yeah, but the four of you all live together.' I know I'm giving him an excuse and not the truth, but I don't want to even think about the truth right now because it kind of hurts.

'You want us to all get a place?' Seth asks as we shuffle off the curb and cross the street to the quaint-looking coffeehouse that has one of the best mocha cappuccinos I've ever had.

I shake my head. 'Six people under one roof is too much.'

'Good, because I really didn't want to,' he says with a playful nudge in my side. 'I just didn't want to seem like a jerk.'

'You're not a jerk,' I tell him as I jump up onto the curb. 'You're the bestest friend ever.'

'You're so right.' He points a finger at me. 'Just like I'm so right about needing to talk to him, see where your future lies.' He steers us around a car pulling out of the coffee shop. 'I love the boy to death, but he needs to start expressing how he feels more instead of always leaving you guessing.'

'Kayden's good to me,' I say defensively. 'But he's had a lot of stuff happen to him and it makes it hard for him to trust people, I think.'

Annoyance fills Seth's expression. 'So have you, and that's something you both need to remember.'

'Seth, please just drop it, okay?' I hope he can't read me as well as he usually does because I don't want to talk about this.

He studies me suspiciously. 'You're keeping something from me,' he says as we arrive at the coffee shop, but instead of walking in, he stops just before we reach the door and makes me stop with him. 'Okay, Miss Callie, fess up. What aren't you telling me?'

A stray strand of my bangs falls into my face as I try to keep my gaze averted from him, but I've never been a good liar and end up breaking down beneath his withering stare within seconds.

'Okay, fine.' I blow out a breath as I look at Seth. 'I do know for sure that Kayden doesn't want to live with me because I asked him at the beginning of the year.'

'What!' Seth exclaims, dropping his hold on me. 'Why am I hearing about this now?'

I inch toward the railing as someone walks out of the door to the coffeehouse. 'Because I didn't really feel like talking about it.'

He frowns as he puts his elbows on the railing and reclines against it. 'Well, what exactly did Kayden say? Just straight up no, I don't want to live with you?'

'Well, he didn't straight up say it like that,' I explain. 'I just said something about how it'd be cool to live in an apartment with a roommate next semester and how I was thinking about it, but I needed a roommate . . . and he didn't say anything.'

Seth relaxes and shakes his head, restraining a grin. 'My dear, darling, naive Callie. Implying something isn't the same as asking.' He pats my head like I'm a child. 'And when it comes to guys, you have to make sure to be really straightforward with what you want. Trust me, I have to deal with it all the time with Greyson.'

'Yeah, you're probably right.' I move back as he reaches around me and opens the door for me to go inside. 'It's just really hard putting myself out there like that because, what if he does give me a flat-out no?'

Seth follows me inside then lets the door go, shutting out the cold. The air smells like fresh coffee and cinnamon and the sounds of clicking keyboards flutter around us, since many students come here with their laptops for the free Wi-Fi.

'I don't think he will,' Seth says as we get in line.

I stare at the menu above the countertop, trying to figure out what to order. 'I'm not so sure . . .' I step forward with the line. 'He's been really sad and kind of distant lately.'

'Then ask him why. Callie, come on. I know this is your first relationship, but you guys are close enough that there shouldn't be space between you.' When I start to open my mouth to protest, he adds, 'Hey, you have to listen to me. I'm now officially a psych major and know what I'm talking about.'

I choke on a laugh. 'I hate to break it to you, but just because you're majoring in psychology doesn't mean you know everything. The classes don't teach you everything.'

'I know that.' He puts two fingers to his temple. 'It's this bad boy right here that makes me so damn insightful.'

I shake my head, but smile. Regardless of Seth being a know-it-all right now, he is right – I do need to talk to Kayden.

'All right, I'll do it.'

'You better. And besides, living in an apartment is way, way better than living in the dorms. And you can be super noisy whenever you want.' He waggles his eyebrows at me.

Despite my blush, I decide to play along. 'Oh, I know. That's the main reason I want to move in with Kayden – so I can have some alone time without worrying about roommates walking in on us.'

He gives me the biggest grin ever. 'Look at my baby girl; all grown up.'

I stand up straighter. 'Now if I could just get the balls to ask Kayden.'

Seth's face turns red as he works to stifle his laughter, but it gets the best of him and he hurries and places his hand over his mouth. 'I cannot believe you just said balls.'

'You know what?' I say as we reach the register. 'I can believe it. I'm not the same girl I used to be.'

He lowers his hand from his mouth and the humor dissolves from his expression. 'You're so right. You have changed. You're so much stronger now.'

Even though it's our turn to order, we give each other a hug. 'We've both come so far,' I tell him because Seth has had his own struggles as well and yet here we are – happy, healthy, and enjoying life. Survivors, that's what we are. I just wish Kayden could see that about himself. Realize just how far he's come.

Maybe Seth's right. Maybe it's time to grab that little space between Kayden and me. After all, I have faced worse than asking my boyfriend to move in with me. Way, way worse.

Chapter 2

#107 Have a Winter Wonderland Magical Moment.

Kayden

I've been in a downer of a mood lately. It's nowhere near the same as it used to be when I'd get so down I'd lock myself in the bathroom and cut out the pain by slicing my own skin open and letting myself bleed. I won't go back to that place no matter what happens to me. I refuse to live in that dark hole ever again. I want things to remain light. I just wish I could fully grab onto it like Callie grabs life, but there's some things – fears – holding me back. An abundance of things bothering me when I really start to analyze it. Like the fact that Thanksgiving is in less than a month, making it almost a year since my father stabbed me then bailed with my mother before he could pay the consequences. It was the year when my already crumbling life fell apart. The year when I just about gave up and ended it all.

But I didn't. I survived and I should be grateful – which I am – but it still bothers me that my father and mother are who knows where, doing who knows what, maybe without a care in the world.

Then there's the fact that my oldest brother, Dylan, invited me to his house for Thanksgiving to a *family* dinner. I'm not sure what to do with that one, how to react to the word *family*. I can't even picture the concept of sitting around the table with my brother and his wife and all of her family, laughing and chatting while we stuff our stomachs with food. Dylan said he would have invited Tyler, too, but neither of us has seen him in quite a while, and we worry that he's addicted to drugs, living on the streets somewhere like he's done in the past. Or worse, maybe he's not alive at all.

I feel like I'm stuck in the past, and I want to move forward. My therapist tells me I need to all the time. But it's more complicated than it seems and depressing to take in sometimes – the lack of family I have and the fact that I'll never truly have a group of people there for me.

There is one person who always gets me through my despair, though.

Callie Lawrence.

She's the best thing that's ever happened to me. My ray of sunshine through the rain, the clouds, the storm that's hovered over my head. She can make me smile when I'm down, laugh when I'm unhappy. She's the one person who has ever loved me, and who I completely and wholly love back in a way I can barely understand sometimes.

I honestly thought I could never love anyone the way I love her. That I'd never know how to love since I never really learned how to. However, Callie showed me how to open my heart – at least, when it comes to loving her. She makes it so easy and sometimes it confuses me because why couldn't my family just do it – love each other instead of being so full of ugly hatred?

'Kayden, get your head in the practice!' my coach hollers as he waves at me to get my ass on the field. I've been standing on the sidelines, staring at the end field for who knows how long, lost in my thoughts.

Getting my head back into practice mode, I jog into the center of the field, hooking the chin strap as I join my other teammates in the huddle. We're in our practice uniforms, the field icy from last night's intense temperature drop, and it's still fucking cold. But it's good to be outdoors, distracting myself from the thoughts that haunt me whenever I'm in my room alone. Playing clears my head more than anything else, except for maybe talking to Callie, who I get to see when practice is over.

Still, even when I'm playing, I can hear *his* faint voice telling me what to do. It's always there whenever I'm doing anything athletic and sometimes when I'm asleep. I hate that I hear it, but after years of it being drilled in my mind, I can't get rid of the sound.

Run.

Do better.

Go faster.

Play harder.

Keep going until you break.

It's only when I'm dripping with sweat and completely in the game that I can barely hear my father's voice in my head, my heart thudding too loud to hear anything but the overworked beat of it. It makes me love/hate football – love it for me, but hate it because of him.

Still, I focus on what I need to do for practice, putting my heart into playing well, running the drills, throwing, catching, playing as good as I always do. By the time we're finished and I'm heading to the locker room, the sweat has soaked through my uniform and my brain is too exhausted to think, so I'm feeling pretty good. Coach pulls me aside before I go inside and tells me how good I'm doing, but then gives me some things to work on. He usually does this, but he's been on my case a lot this year since we've been playing so well. There's been a lot of talk about my future in football, even though I'm still a sophomore and still have a ways to go before the draft comes into my sights. I'm grateful for the time, too, because I'm not even sure what I want to do anyway.

My whole life my dad threw me into sports and I always excelled at them, so it just seemed like that was the path I'd follow. And I love playing, but sometimes I wonder if there's more to life than this. If maybe there's something out there for me that's not connected to my father's dream for me and the sound of his voice constantly haunting me with every run and throw I make.

After I go to the locker room, I take a quick shower and change into a pair of jeans and a T-shirt. Then I slip my jacket on and head out to my car in the parking lot. It's not the best-looking car in the world, but it's better than my motorcycle and gets me to places. Plus, the great part is I bought it myself, from the part-time job I have at the local gym. It's all mine; my own little pride and joy. Not my father's.

I climb inside and rev up the engine, tossing my bag into the backseat. It's getting late; the sun has gone behind the mountains, so I turn on the headlights and push the car into drive. I'm about to pull out of the lot when I get a text message, my phone buzzing in my pocket

Pressing on the brake, I stop the car near the exit to take my phone out of my pocket, smiling because I know who the text is from before I even check it.

Callie: Hey! Where r u? I thought we were supposed to meet at your dorm at seven, but you're not here . . .

Me: Sorry, I'm running a little late. Coach wanted to talk about stuff.

I frown at the intentional avoidance of the subject. I haven't talked to Callie about the uncertainty of my future in football – or the uncertainty in my future, period. She's always so positive and knows exactly what she wants out of life; it makes it difficult to talk to someone who knows what they want.

Me: R u at my dorm right now?

Callie: Yeah, in your room . . . Niko let me in.

I pull a face at the mention of my roommate. Not that I don't like him or anything, but he has some serious issues and he's high half the damn time.

Kayden: Is he with you right now?

Callie: No, he just left . . . why?

Kayden: Just wondering . . . I'm heading there now. Be there in like 10.

Callie: K :) And I have something really important I want to talk to you about . . . It's about us.

I grow uneasy, wondering what it is, that she might want to take a break from us or something else equally as bad. I really don't think that is it, but my mind always seems to go to that dark place whenever there's an unknown in front of me. I can't help worrying Callie will hurt me because she has the power to. She owns my heart and soul completely and she could easily break it.

Lost in my worries, I pull out onto the road and drive toward my dorm building. By the time I'm parking the car, it's snowing like a blizzard. Massive snowflakes splatter against the windshield and instantly soak through my clothes as I hop out and jog across the frosted grass to the entrance doors. I breathe in the warmth as I step into the foyer area.

23

It's nearing Halloween and everything is decorated in black and orange, fake spider webs everywhere, along with this stupid skeleton that makes spooky noises every time someone walks by. There are a few people sitting around in the lounging area, laughing and talking, a couple of whom I know, so I give them a wave and say hello before going to the elevator.

The closer I get to my room, the more eager I get to touch Callie, wishing I could do it all the time. Unfortunately, I'm not in the same dorm building as her and it makes staying together all night a bit of a pain in the ass. Honestly, it'd be easier if we just lived together, but that is one hell of a big step and I'm not sure if I'm – we're – ready for that or if she'd even want to.

When I arrive at my room, I punch in the code and walk in, smiling even before I see her. But then I frown the moment I step over the threshold when I discover the room is empty; just two unmade twin beds, some empty Dorito bags, and a lot of Coke cans on the floor, which makes me miss Luke as a roommate and his need to keep everything clean and organized. There's also a stack of DVDs on my nightstand, which I'm assuming Callie brought over since they weren't here earlier.

I'm scratching my head, wondering where she went when my phone vibrates from inside my pocket. My eyebrows knit as I take it out and swipe my finger across the screen.

Callie: Put your coat on and meet me outside on the east side of the campus yard.

Me: Why does this sound so suspicious . . . you're not planning my murder, r u?

Callie: Not tonight. I saved my roll of duct tape and shovel for another time ;)

I can't help but chuckle at her adorableness.

Me: All right, just as long as no shovel and tape are involved, I'll b out in a few :)

Callie: k, see ya soon :)

I stuff my phone back into my pocket, wondering what she's up to. She's been so happy lately, even with the fact that Caleb – the guy who raped her when she was twelve – is still out there somewhere in the world, living his life, without paying for what he did, not just to Callie, but Luke's sister as well, along with a few others. He likely won't ever have to pay for what he did to them. He'll go on living his life, doing whatever he wants, while his victims are left to cope with the destruction. A huge flaw in life and one I understand way too well.

Shaking the depressing thought from my head, I

Shaking the depressing thought from my head, I tug my beanie over my brown hair before I depart toward the cold again. I try to stay upbeat as I take the elevator to the bottom floor, go back outside, and wind around the building, heading to the side where Callie instructed me to go. The leafless trees around the building are decorated with lights that reflect against the ice covering everything. It's freaking freezing out here, my breath puffing out in a cloud in front of my face. I should have worn a heavier coat. But once I step out into the open area on the east side between a few benches and rows of trees, I stop caring that I'm outdoors and freezing my ass off.

Callie is standing in the middle of the frosted trees and lights, staring down at the ground. She has her head tipped down, her coat zipped up to her chin, and she's kicking at the snow with the tip of her boot. Her hood is down and snowflakes dot her long brown hair, but she doesn't seem to mind, lost in her thoughts.

She's beautiful.

Amazing.

Perfect.

I give myself a moment to appreciate everything that's her before I walk toward her and make my presence known. She must hear my boots crunch against the snow because her gaze lifts and finds me before I reach her. Snow dots her eyelashes, her cheeks are flushed, and she has a smile on her face, her eyes so full of love I seriously nearly turn around and look over my shoulder to make sure there's no one else standing there that she could be looking at.

'Hey you,' she says, still grinning at me. Then she shifts her weight and a hint of her nerves slips through, which makes me nervous as well.

Why would she be nervous?

'Hey you, back.' My feet move toward her on their own, wanting – needing – to be near her. 'Why are you standing out here in the freezing cold?'

She holds up her finger, indicating to wait just a second. Then she glances at the leafless, snow-bitten tree beside her before she ducks behind it. A heartbeat later, music envelops me. When she steps back out from behind the tree, she's smiling as the snowflakes swirl around us, almost moving with the slow rhythm of the song.

'What do you have back there?' I ask. 'An iPod dock or something?'

She shakes her head as she hikes through the snow toward me, reducing the space between us, something I'm ridiculously grateful for. In fact, I want it all gone

– not a single drop of space left between our bodies.

'No, it's Luke's stereo. Seth borrowed it from him so I could use it for this.'

My smile rises, the first time I've smiled all day. 'God, he's so weird with all that old crap he keeps around, right?'

'Like all his mix tapes?' she says with a soft laugh as she stops in front of me and tips her head back to look up at me.

I eliminate the rest of the space between us and put my hands on her hips. Suddenly, I become warm in the midst of the cold. 'I seriously think he belongs in the eighties.'

'Maybe he does.' She loops her arms around the back of my neck and draws me closer. 'What era do you think we'd belong in if we could go live in a different one?'

I consider what she said. 'How about the sixties?'

She beams up at me. 'We'd be all about the peace, love, and happiness.'

'I think that sounds a lot like you.' I tuck a strand of her damp hair behind her ear. 'I'm not sure about me, though.'

Her forehead creases as I stroke her cheek with my finger, mesmerized by the softness of her skin. I've touched it a thousand times, yet every time is as amazing as the first.

'You've seemed a little bit down lately. Has something been bothering you?'

'I've just been thinking about some stuff.' I trace a path up her jawline to her temple.

'About family stuff?'

'Yeah . . . I can't help it . . . with the holidays coming. It's just got me thinking.'

'About your family?'

I swallow the stupid lump that has wedged its way up my throat. 'Yeah, about my lack of one.' I don't really mean to say it because I don't want to be a downer when clearly she had some sort of fun night planned, but it just slips out.

'You have me,' she says quietly, placing a hand on my stubbly cheek. 'You always will.'

My heart tightens in my chest. 'I know I do,' I say, wishing it were that simple, that I did fully believe she'd always be here with me, that nothing would change, and that that could be enough in life. But I've been abandoned before, so there's a bit of a skeptic in me.

Still, being here with her momentarily lifts my problems away, and I lean in to kiss her, unable to take the space between us any longer. However, she pulls away, stopping mid-kiss, and leaving me panting for air.

'What's wrong?' I ask.

She lets out a shaky breath, jittery and shivering from the cold. 'I have to ask you something . . . something really, really important.'

I search her eyes and I see the same nerves I noticed when I first walked up to her. 'What's wrong?'

She takes another unsteady breath and her hold on me tightens, her fingers digging into the fabric of my coat, like she's afraid to let me go. 'Okay, so I have something I want you to think about, but I don't want you to answer it tonight.'

'Okay . . .?' I'm trying not to get worried, but it's hard when she's acting this way.

Her eyes are wide and full of terror, but she refuses to look away from me. 'Okay, so I've been thinking a lot about our . . . our living situation.' Her chest rapidly rises and falls, causing a cloud of fog to rise around her face. 'Remember how at the beginning of the school year I mentioned something about how much easier it'd be if we were living together?'

I waver, because I really don't remember what she's talking about, but it seems like maybe I should. 'I

30

vaguely remember you saying something about you wanting to move out of the dorm and get your own apartment.'

A loud exhale puffs from her lips. 'Well, what I meant to say when I said it . . . or what I should have just flat out said is that maybe we should just . . . you and I,' she gestures between the two of us, 'live . . . together . . .' She trails off, biting her lip, which has turned a bit blue from the cold.

I swallow hard, unsure how to answer. I have no idea how I feel about the idea. Excitement. Want. God, the want. But I'm fucking conflicted because within the want there's a fear. Am I ready for that?

Yes.

No.

Yes.

No.

Maybe.

Shit.

Why can't I just give her what she wants?

She deserves that.

Deserves more.

I'm feeling way too much at the moment. The old Kayden would be bailing out by now and running back to his room to find a razor because it'd be the easiest way to deal with this – or not deal with it anyway. But I don't want to be that guy – become that guy again.

Callie watches me with hope in her eyes while I struggle to sort through all the confusion flowing through my mind. My lips part to try to explain to her what's going on, even though I'm guessing it's going to be a jumble of nonsense, but she quickly covers my mouth with her hand.

'Don't answer me right now.' She slowly lowers her hand from my lips. 'Just think about it. Talk to your therapist and figure out if you really want to do it or not,' she says with a shrug. 'I was just letting you know that I want to.'

I nod, letting out a breath trapped inside my chest. 'Okay, I'll think about it.'

Her lips curve into a smile then she stands on her tiptoes to place a kiss on my mouth. Her taste drowns me, and for the slightest, liberating moment, I forget about everything. The kiss is too quick, though, and when she starts to pull away, I cup the back of her neck and pull her right back to me, refusing to let her go, wanting to feel the calmness inside me just a little bit longer.

She doesn't protest as I slide my tongue deep inside

her mouth, exploring every inch of it as I grasp onto her hips, gripping her sides. She clutches onto me tightly too, our bodies aligning as snow falls around us, soaks through our clothes to our skin while soft music continues to play in the background.

It's one of those easy moments with her that I look forward to and I wish I could stay in forever. But for some reason I have a feeling the snow is going to stop falling and life will move on.

Moving forward.

To a future.

I just wish I knew what the hell I was supposed to do.

Chapter 3

#117 Don't Let the Cursor Torture You.

Callie

It's getting close to Halloween and I want to dress up for it. I haven't actually dressed up since I was eleven, the last time I felt like a child. I know I'm not a child now, but having my childhood stolen so early from me, I want to have some fun. And Seth wants me to go to a Halloween concert thingy with Greyson, him, Luke, and Violet. A couples' Halloween/dance/costume concert. I agree, but tell him I'll have to talk to Kayden, unsure if it's his kind of thing.

I like the idea too much probably and shouldn't get my hopes up until I know for sure if he'll go, but I never got to do the whole prom thing, never got to wear something that made me look pretty, didn't really believe I was pretty, nor did I want to be at the time or want to draw that kind of attention. I never got to dance with a guy who I loved and who looked at me like I was the most beautiful thing in the world. And I want it for just one night.

Seth coaxes me into going shopping for a costume before I get the chance to ask Kayden, but I don't mind. In fact, I'm having fun looking for something to wear. Although Seth seems to think he needs to put in his two cents, and let's just say that his costume ideas are . . . well, a little bit too daring and bold for my taste.

'Yeah, I'm not sure Kayden would go for the whole Peter Pan/Tinkerbell thing,' I tell Seth when he holds up a costume that includes green tights and curly-toed shoes.

He gives me an innocent smile, shoving the costume at me. 'Why ever not?'

I roll my eyes as I continue to search the rack in front of me. 'Um, because it includes tights. That's why.' I move hangers to the side as I look through the choices. 'Besides, I don't want to be Tinkerbell.'

Seth frowns disappointedly. 'Yeah, but Kayden wears those super-tight pants when he's playing football, which is pretty much the same as tights.'

I laugh as I sift through the very slutty-looking options of costumes, something I'm not ready for, nor do I ever think I'll be ready for. Again, I just don't think it's in my personality. 'Yeah, and I've caught you checking him out before in those super-tight pants, buddy. You are so not as discreet as you think.'

'Who says I was trying to be discreet?' he says, putting his hand on his hip. 'I was just admiring the view. And don't pretend like you don't do it, too – admire a nice ass when you see one.'

My cheeks warm and he laughs at me, amused by my embarrassment. Still chuckling, he wanders around the racks filling the small store, searching for a costume. The selection is pretty picked over and there are a lot of people here skimming through the already limited supply. There's some Halloween-type music playing through the speakers to add to the scary decorations of bats, witches, and ghosts.

'So have you decided on one yet?' Seth asks, backing away from the rack and rubbing his stomach. 'Because I'm getting super hungry.'

I shake my head as I pull a face at a thin piece of leather that's supposed to be some sort of dress, yet looks more like a really short shirt. 'The problem is I don't want to be something scary or slutty and that's all they really have here.'

He glances over at the wall of masks, then the rack I was just looking through. 'That sort of eliminates a lot of options, if not all of them.'

'I know,' I sigh, glancing around the store. 'I just want to be something pretty. Something that's not slutty, but is sort of sexy in a way where I don't have to show a lot of skin, if that makes any sense. Something that will . . . dazzle Kayden.' I grin at my word usage because dazzle is one of Seth's favorite words.

He bobs his head up and down to the music as he looks around the store contemplatively. 'That actually makes perfect sense for you.' He takes my hand. 'Come with me, beautiful; I think I have an idea for the perfect thing for you. One that will make you' – he grins at me – 'dazzle the whole entire world.'

I smile as I follow him out of the store, hoping that today's efforts will be worth it, that maybe somehow I can make the night magical, or at least get Kayden to smile. That alone would make all efforts worth it.

Later that day, I return to my dorm room with a bag that's holding what I think will be the perfect costume. I know I'm being silly, that I'm almost twenty and should not be getting excited over a silly party, but I am.

Last Halloween, Kayden and I weren't technically boyfriend and girlfriend. Yeah, we were hanging out, but that was about it. And about a month later, around Thanksgiving, everything fell apart when Kayden beat up Caleb for what he did to me and then his father beat up him and stabbed him for getting in trouble with the police over it. It was a terrible, horrible time. I know Kayden still thinks about it a lot, even though he doesn't talk to me about it too much. So I want the end of this year and future ones to be fun. Plain and simple fun.

After I put my bags away, I turn on my iPod, hitting random before popping my headphones on. 'Winter Song' by Sara Bareilles and Ingrid Michaelson clicks on, totally fitting for the storm outside. Then I get my laptop from the nightstand and plop down onto the bed.

I do a little writing for my internship, but after getting bored with it I change documents and work on one of my Advance Fiction projects for my end-of-the-year portfolio. The theme is fiction, but Professor Gladsyman pressed that we should write about something that feels real, something that's resting on the line between fiction and nonfiction.

Sometimes, I feel . . .

Yeah, that's all I have so far. It's not like I'm having writer's block. Okay, well maybe I do, but it's not only that. Writing the vague truth, that's the hard part. But I'm not even supposed to be writing the truth, am I? Honestly, I'm kind of confused which route I'm supposed to go, especially since the professor kept making air quotes whenever he said fiction. I swear he wanted us to read his mind or something to figure out what he wanted.

Sighing, I delete my whole three words and then take up the hobby of staring at the blank, white screen and that damn blinking cursor, the one that I swear is whispering, *you better find an idea,* over and over again, not to encourage me – to torture me. Every time I try to get it to stop, the voice only grows louder and I swear to God I'm going crazy – writer crazy.

After a while, I get up and get a snack from my dresser drawer then I take out my dress – aka my costume – and admire it again, totally procrastinating.

When I'd tried the dress on in the store, I'd felt like a gothic princess. Yeah, it was a cliché – well, minus the gothic part – but I welcomed it, remembering how I used to dream of being a princess and going to prom before it got squashed. After I was raped, I shut down completely, living only within myself. I chopped off my hair and only spoke to my journal for the most part, everything I was feeling pouring out through that pen. That's what I did until I left for college, which means I convinced myself all that high-school stuff was silly when really I wanted to go. Never happened.

'It could be like prom for you,' Seth had said when he was trying to convince me that this was indeed what I needed to wear. 'And you could be like Cinderella and lose your glass slipper so Kayden has to find you and give it back.'

I'd been holding the dress up to myself and gazing at my reflection in the store's mirror. 'Seth, this is just a party. And this is definitely not a dress Cinderella would wear.'

'Then be Callierella,' he said with a wink. 'Or Calliepunzel and you can lock yourself in your bedroom until Kayden begs for you to let him in.'

I had snorted a laugh. 'Are you drunk? I mean, I know you had a margarita at lunch, but it usually takes a lot more for you to get tipsy.'

'I'm not drunk,' he said, snatching the dress from my hand. 'I'm just trying to give you the fairytale you deserve.'

'Life isn't a fairytale,' I replied. But in the end, I bought the dress, kind of wishing it was.

If life were a fairytale, I think to myself as I hang the dress up in the closet, *it would be dark and twisted a lot. Then again, some of those fairytales do have a dark side, an evil villain, a wicked dilemma to get over, like a curse. But I would never want to be a princess, at least the kind that waits around for a prince to save them.*

I'd want to save myself. And maybe the prince as well. Maybe we could save each other together.

An idea sparkles inside my mind and I let out an excited clap and cheer. 'Holy crap, I've got it!'

Right then, Harper enters the room with a bag slung over her shoulder. She gives me this weird look as she sets her things down on the dresser and her bag on the bed. *You okay?* she mouths because I have my headphones in.

I nod eagerly as I skip back to my bed. 'Yeah, just got a really cool idea.' Then I turn to the computer and place my fingers on the keyboard, listening to the voice inside my head that doesn't belong to a cursor, but a character, as I type the first three words.

The Truthful Fairytale.

Chapter 4

#102 Don't Let Your Family Get to You.

Kayden

Working at the gym isn't what I want to do for the rest of my life, but it gives me a cash flow. It's loud and always has this weird smell I never notice when I'm working out but can barely breathe through when I'm working. It usually takes me at least an hour before my nostrils get used to it. Today, though, it's giving me a headache, or maybe that's just because I didn't sleep very well last night. I want to lie down on the floor and go to sleep, but instead I have to stand at the front counter for four hours straight and talk to people when they need help.

My phone's been buzzing in my pocket all day, but I can't answer it until my break. I think it might be

Callie, and it's driving me insane because I want to talk to her, yet I don't. After our conversation the other day about moving in, I've been worried about what she'll say, afraid she's going to ask me what my decision is and I'm going to have to tell her I have no clue. My only hope left is to maybe sort out my jumbled thoughts at my therapy appointment tomorrow.

Finally, at a little after two o'clock, I get my break. After putting on my jacket, I step out the back door and into the cold. The sky is grey and the snow is refusing to stop or melt, piling up on the roads. I wonder just how intense the winter's going to be. Usually it doesn't even start snowing until November, but it's the end of October and there's already a shitload.

My phone vibrates again and I cut across the icy parking lot toward my car as I rummage around in my pocket for it. I'm getting ready to dial Callie's number when I see the screen and realize all the missed calls aren't from her but from my older brother Dylan.

'That's fucking weird,' I mutter, retrieving the keys from my pocket as I reach my car. Dylan and I talk about once a week, but usually if I miss his call, he doesn't call back until a few days later. Today, however, he's tried to call over eight times and sent one text.

Dylan: Call me ASAP.

I dial his number as I hop into my car and turn the engine on, cranking up the heater with the phone pressed to my ear.

'Hey,' he answers with an edge to his voice. 'I was actually going to try to call you again.'

'Yeah, I was at work,' I reply, staring out the window. 'What's up?'

'Nothing . . . well, everything.' He hesitates, then sighs. 'It's about Tyler.'

My heart rate quickens at the mention of my other brother's name. 'What happened to him?'

Dylan sighs again and it's more weighted this time. 'I got a call from him a few days ago, and he said he needed help, that he's been living on the streets. I could tell he was ripped out of his mind – could barely understand half the words he said.'

'Living on the streets where exactly?'

'I'm not sure yet. Haven't gotten that far with him.' Dylan sighs for the third time and I know it's bad. Whatever's going on, it's really, really bad. 'He was actually headed up to Virginia when he called me. I guess he found out where I lived and started hitch-hiking to my place. He was strung out and we're trying to help him detox right now, but I'm not sure how well it's going to work.'

'Where was he hitchhiking from?' I dare ask, wondering if it's from wherever my parents are. And what if it is? What does that mean? That they'll be entering Dylan's life again, too? Will he let them?

A thousand questions race through my mind as Dylan answers, 'I have no idea. Somewhere down south, I think, but he acts like he can't remember.'

I grip onto the steering wheel, attempting to control the frustration stirring inside me, but I've never been great at controlling my emotions and I start to sweat from the anxiousness I'm feeling. 'Or maybe he does, but he's not saying because Mom and Dad told him not to.'

'Yeah, I kind of wondered the same thing. Been wondering it for the few months after you got ahold of me and told me what'd been going on, but then again, Tyler is, well, Tyler. And he might just have been living on the streets so fucking high he really can't remember where he was.'

'Yeah, I guess so.' Dylan's right. Tyler could easily have just wandered in from off the streets, but part of me wants it to be the other way around, wants him to know where they are. I don't know why, though. It's not like I want them back in my life. I don't even want to see them again unless it's seeing my dad behind bars. Just like his father – my grandfather – is now.

'I know what you're thinking, Kayden,' Dylan says, interrupting my thoughts. 'And you need to stop thinking about that. You need to try to let it go. Don't worry about Mom and Dad anymore.'

'I'm not worrying about them,' I lie and well, too. I've always been good at lying, which isn't a good thing, but it's something I had to learn how to do at an early age when people would ask about my bruises and broken bones.

'Well, I didn't really mean worry. More like, letting them get to you.'

'I'm fine. Really,' I lie again. I don't feel fine. I feel angry. All the time.

'Are you still seeing your therapist?' he asks cautiously.

'Yeah.' I turn down the heater. 'Once a week, every week.'

'Good. I think it's good for you. I still see mine sometimes when things get bad, like the other day when I had to pick Tyler up.' When I don't say anything, not sure what to say, he changes the subject. 'But anyway, I just wanted to call and let you know what's up. We might check Tyler into a rehab if we can get him to commit, so he might be around for Thanksgiving when you come out.'

I frown. 'Thanksgiving?'

'Yeah, you're coming up, right?' he asks. 'I mean, I thought that's what you said.'

What I said was I'd think about it, but I still mutter, 'Yeah, I guess.'

My lungs begin to constrict as I think about last Thanksgiving and what happened. It'd started out okay, getting to spend time with Callie, and then we'd had sex for the first time. But things got ugly from then on, a beautiful moment tainted by reality.

'Look, I got to go. My break's over,' I lie to Dylan for the third time during this conversation. 'But let me know what happens with Tyler.'

'I will.' He hesitates as I turn off the engine and get out of the car. 'And Kayden, just so you know, he's been asking about you – what you're doing, if you're okay. He keeps saying he wants to talk to you, but I'm not going to let him until he sobers, just to make sure he doesn't say . . . well, anything that isn't meant to be said.' I think he might be trying to protect me, but I'm not sure, since no one has ever really done that for me before, at least no one in my family. 'And you only have to talk to him if you want to.'

I'm unsure how to respond. Dylan and I have been getting along okay, but right now he's showing a lot of emotion directed toward me. It's strange and unfamiliar, especially since I spent a lot of time thinking that he hated me when I was a kid, after he took off when he was eighteen and left me with our dad and mom, never so much as even calling to say where he was living. It's something we haven't really talked about too much either, although my therapist thinks it might be healthy for us to do so. However, I don't want to go down that road yet – open up those old scars that are still trying to heal.

'Okay . . . thanks for letting me know,' I say awkwardly as I shut the car door then lock it because it's too old school for a key fob.

'Yeah, no problem,' he replies, sounding uncomfortable himself. I hear someone say something in the background and he quickly says, 'Oh, and Liz wants to know if you're bringing anyone here for Thanksgiving with you.'

I want to tell him I haven't even fully committed to coming yet, but instead say, 'I'm not sure, but I'll let you know soon.'

'Okay, but just so you know, we'd love to have you and Callie here if she can come.' He sounds like he means it.

Again, I'm a little thrown off by this weird I-care-for-you thing he's got going. I keep my composure, though, and say goodbye before heading back to work, even though I have ten more minutes of break time. I try not to think about Tyler too much, yet I can't help it. Because what if he really does know.

Knows where my father is.

Chapter 5

#134 Invite Someone to Prom **coughs** aka Halloween Party.

Callie

'Really?' I say to Seth as I read what he just wrote on my whiteboard. Seth and I have been creating this to-do list since the beginning of freshman year when we first became friends. There's no rule to what goes on there, it just needs to be something we think at least one of us has to try. This whiteboard version actually starts at one hundred since the list got so long we had to transfer some of them onto a piece of paper.

'Yes, really.' He taps the marker against number one hundred seventeen. 'It isn't any weirder than this one.'

'Hey, I totally did that the other day.' I snatch the marker from his hand and draw a line through number one hundred seventeen.

'You're so weird,' he says as I put the cap of the marker back on and toss it aside.

I roll my eyes at him. 'That's the pot calling the kettle black.'

'Totally,' he agrees, his gaze drifting to the window. 'So are you ready for this?'

My face bunches up in confusion. 'Ready for what?'

He taps his finger against the whiteboard right where he just wrote one hundred thirty-four. 'Duh, what you're going to do today.'

Shaking my head, I sink down on the bed. 'I'm not doing that.'

He puts his hands on his hips and stares me down. 'You so are.'

I fold my arms and aim a challenging look at him. 'Am not.'

'You have to,' he insists. 'The concert is tomorrow and I already told Greyson you were coming.'

'Fine, I'll ask Kayden,' I tell him, defeated. 'But not in some weird, cheesy prom way like people do in high school.'

'You so are, Callie Lawrence.' He grabs my arm and

jerks me to my feet so hard I stumble. 'This is something you so need to do.'

I give him the nastiest look ever. I get that he thinks I need to relive my high school days, since they sucked big time, and I want to, but at the same time . . . 'I'm afraid I'll be living in the past if I do it.'

His determination softens, but he still pulls me to the door, throwing my coat at me in the process. 'Nope. Not at all.' He opens the door and steers me out into the hallway with him, navigating us around a group of people loitering in the hallways. 'See, this is you and me walking away from the past and heading to the future.'

'You're speaking metaphorically, aren't you?' I ask as we reach the elevator and he presses the down button.

'I had my Philosophy class today,' he admits as the elevator doors slide open and we step inside. 'Now, would you pretty please do this with me?' His finger hovers over the button of the ground floor, waiting for me to agree because in the end, regardless of how pushy he is, he'll always back down if I ask him to. That's the thing with Seth and why he's such a good friend.

'Oh, fine. Let's go be cheesy,' I huff as if I'm aggravated, but in the end we are both smiling. And really, that's kind of the point of this, of anything, isn't it?

'So this is what people do when they ask each other to prom, huh?' I stare at the front of Kayden's lofty dorm building as Seth snaps a thin branch from the tree, causing a pile of snow to fall on his head.

Sweeping the snow out of his hair, he nods then he crouches down and draws a heart in the snow. 'Yes, you have to be creative with these things. In fact, the more creative, the better.' As he says it, he writes in the snow:

Kayden, will you go to a Halloween concert with me? I would swoon over the moon if you did.

He stands up with a proud expression after he finishes. 'See, now all you have to do is go get him.' He drops the branch and dusts snow from his gloves.

'*Swoon over the moon?*' I question and he gives me a *what* look. I retrieve my gloves from my pocket and slip my fingers inside them. 'I have a better idea.' I pick up the branch and brush my hands across the surface of the snow, erasing what he wrote and giggling when he starts to complain. Then I kneel down and write something that's actually from me.

'If I'm going to do this, then I should do it,' I tell

him as I trace the tip of the stick across the snow. When I'm done, I stand up and admire my handiwork.

Seth steps beside me and reads what I wrote. '*Kayden, let me dazzle you at a Halloween concert. P.S. Seth made me do this because he put it on the list.*' He gives me a look. 'That's really what you want to write?'

I brush snow out of my hair that's falling from the trees. 'Yep, I think it's perfect.'

He sighs, but he's smiling, so I know he thinks I'm amusing. 'Here, let me see your phone.'

I reach into my pocket and give it to him, not really thinking too much about it. 'Why? Where's yours?'

He's chuckling under his breath as he types something. 'In my pocket.'

'Then why do you need mine.'

Laughing, he tosses me the phone. 'Let me know how it goes and if you need a ride later.' He saunters off toward the parking lot.

'Seth, what did you do?' I shout at him, but then shake my head at myself and go into my text messages to see for myself. '*Hey, lover. Meet me outside your dorm building in ten. I have a naughty little surprise for you.*' I read it aloud, unsure whether to be angry or amused. I decide to go for the latter, since Seth didn't mean anything by it and Kayden shouldn't think much of it. At least, I hope he doesn't . . . or maybe I do.

Kayden: Hmm . . . I'm intrigued. I'll be down in a sec.

Sighing, I put my phone away and wait for him to come out to me. I wonder if he thinks I'm going to bombard him with another question like I did the other day. I am kind of making it a habit. Texting him to meet me out here in the middle of the yard that looks like a winter wonderland.

I should really find another way to do stuff like this.

A couple of minutes later, Kayden walks outside, stuffing his hands into the pockets of his coat. The wind blows through strands of his brown hair that hangs in his eyes and flips up at his ears. His shoulders are strong, his entire body lean and in shape, but covered in scars, put there by both himself and his father. Still, he's absolutely gorgeous. I've always thought so, even when we were younger. Our parents actually knew each other – small town thing – and had parties a lot that we attended, but Kayden never really noticed me until I stepped in one time right after graduation when his father was in the middle of beating him. It was back when I was still cutting my own hair and wore clothes two sizes too big so I wouldn't get noticed by anyone.

But that night, he noticed me, like I had always noticed him.

And I – neither of us – was the same again.

'You know you can come up to my room?' he teases as he strolls over to me. 'There's not a "no girls allowed" rule.' He winks as he stops in front of me, all smiles. I can see in his eyes that he's keeping something from me, though. Something that's bothering him. It's not even the same sadness I've been seeing for a few weeks. This is different. He's carrying more weight around, like when we first were together and I didn't know about his problems. 'So what's the naughty thing you wanted to show me?' His gaze skims down my body and makes my skin feel like I'm on fire.

'Yeah . . . sorry about that,' I say with an exaggerated sigh. 'Seth actually sent you that text.'

He chuckles under his breath. 'I was kind of wondering.' He looks around at the trees and the parking lot. 'Where is he?'

'Oh, he left,' I tell him as his eyes land back on me. He waits for me to explain so I step back and let him read my little snowflake note.

At first, he appears puzzled, and then he starts to laugh. 'You two are so weird.'

'Yeah, I know . . .' I trail off, wishing I wasn't nervous.

'The thing starts at eight. We can go there or meet up because I know you have practice and stuff.'

He looks back up at me and places his hands on my hips. 'I'd love to go with you, but we'll have to meet there if that's okay? I can't miss practice or coach will fucking flip out.'

The anxiousness in me eases. 'That's perfectly okay. And thank you for going with me. And sorry about the weird note. Seth just thought since I never got to go to prom, this kind of thing would be fun, but not that I think about it. It's kind of weird.' I stop rambling. I don't know why, but I feel stupidly high right now. It's not like we haven't been on dates before – we've been on a ton of them – but this time I'll get to wear the dress I bought. If someone asked me a year ago if I ever thought I'd be excited about doing such a thing, I'd have told them no. But here I am, spreading my wings and flying all on my own.

He gives me a sympathetic look. 'Callie, I'm so sorry . . . that you didn't get to do that stuff.'

'It's not your fault. And besides, you're helping me do that stuff now.'

'Good. I'm glad it feels like I am.' He gives me a sad smile, which I don't like. He's feeling sorry for me and I don't want him to.

'Kayden, it's fine – I'm fine,' I promise him. 'What happened . . . it's in the past and I'm working on moving on – moving forward.'

He looks even sadder, but I'm not sure if it has to do with me anymore. 'Moving forward's good.' He clears his throat then shakes off whatever he's feeling. 'Do I have to dress up, though? For the party?'

I shake my head. 'Not if you don't want to.'

'Are you going to?'

'Yes.'

He momentarily considers something. 'I'll see what I can come up with.'

'Seth wanted you to wear tights,' I tell him, playfully pinching his side. 'And be Peter Pan.'

He swiftly shakes his head. 'No way in hell am I doing that.'

'It's okay,' I assure him. 'I didn't want to be Tinkerbell anyway.'

He nudges my foot with his, his sad mood lightening. 'What are you going to be?'

I wink at him, trying to be suave, but I think it comes off more awkward than anything, but his laugh makes it worth it. 'It's a surprise.'

His eyes search mine and I think he's going to say something deeply profound, like maybe what's got him all down, but then he decides against it. 'You want to come inside? I have Doritos, Coke, and we can stream Netflix.'

'Awe, you know the way to my heart.' My grin breaks through and for a moment, everything feels perfect, if only Kayden could feel it, too. But the hint of sadness in his eyes tells me he doesn't.

Chapter 6

#115 Share a Passionate Dorito/Coke Kiss.

Kayden

I am the shittiest boyfriend in the history of boyfriends. Seriously. Callie is always putting her heart out there for me and I can't even tell her about the call I got from Dylan today. I don't even know why I can't just tell her about it. Or maybe I do. Maybe I know that Callie will make me talk about it because that's the kind of person she is, and I just don't want to talk about it.

After I agree to go to the party/concert with her, we go up to my room. I feel like the biggest douche after her whole statement about prom. I went to every one of mine, did all that stupid shit in high school that was supposed to mean something, but took it for granted. And here Callie is, trying to make up for

60

everything she missed with a Halloween concert, one she asked me to go to. I need to start doing more things for her, making her feel more special, stop being such a shitty boyfriend.

Once we settle on my bed with my laptop in front of us, we pick a movie out, and then binge on snacks and drinks. My roommate is gone so we have the place to ourselves, which usually I'd take advantage of by exploring every inch of Callie's body, but today my head's in a weird place.

Callie must sense my distance too – of course she does – because about halfway through the movie, she moves out of my arms and pauses the screen. 'Okay, what's up?' She grabs a handful of chips and dumps them into her mouth.

'Nothing's up,' I lie, glad the lamp is the only light on so she can't see my face clearly.

She takes a sip of her soda, eyeing me the entire time. 'You know I can tell when you're lying, right?'

I sit up on the bed and rest back against the head-board. 'How?'

She leans over me to set the soda on the nightstand and I breathe in the scent of her hair, strawberries with a hint of vanilla. 'Because your jaw twitches when you're not being honest.'

My fingers absentmindedly travel to my jawline. 'It does not.'

She bites on her lip to keep from grinning. 'Does, too.'

I shake my head as I stretch out my legs. 'Then why haven't you mentioned it before?'

'Because you'd try to control it and I wouldn't have my little secret lie detector anymore,' she says, hitching a leg over me and straddling my lap. 'But I'm calling you out now because I want the truth.' She puts her hands on my chest and lowers her body toward mine, looking me directly in the eye. 'What's bothering you?'

I'm overwhelmed by her nearness and the intensity in her eyes. Even after almost a year of being with her, it still gets under my skin in the best way possible. My head becomes foggy and I find myself divulging without even meaning to.

'I got a call from Dylan today.'

Her legs tighten around me as her muscles tense. 'I know he calls you sometimes, but by your tone . . . I'm guessing it might not have been a normal checking-in call.'

I nod, knowing I have to tell her what happened now; otherwise, I'd be really lying instead of just keeping things to myself. 'It wasn't. He called to tell me that . . .' I clutch onto her hips because touching her makes everything easier. 'That he found Tyler. Or, well, Tyler found him, I guess.'

'What do you mean found? Where was he?'

I shrug. 'Dylan's not sure yet. Tyler's high and I guess he's been living on the street . . .' I trail, still not sure if I believe that story.

'What, you think he might have been living somewhere else and is lying?' Callie asks, reading me like an open book.

I shrug again. 'I'm not sure, but maybe.' I don't want to talk about this anymore and I think she can tell.

'What can I do to make it better?' She places her palm on my cheek and smoothes her thumb along my jawline.

My fingers slip under the bottom of her shirt and caress her soft flesh. 'I can think of a few things.'

A gasp escapes her lips as my fingers drift up her shirt toward her breasts. It's the little noises she makes every time we're together that drive me crazier than anything else. They're what end the moment quicker than I want to because I can't keep myself under control. Just like now.

Tangling my fingers through her hair, I tip her head

back and bring her in for a passionate Dorito/Coke-tasting kiss.

'Kayden,' she groans, her fingers tensing for the briefest moment on my chest, right where my heart is thudding. I know she can feel it, feel what she does to me, and I hope it lets her understand what she means to me.

As my fingers slide beneath her bra and graze her nipple, she instantly surrenders in my arms, opening her mouth and allowing me to deepen the kiss as she rolls her hips against mine. Now I'm the one who's groaning, while tugging at her hair, nipping at her lips, biting her neck, licking her collarbone. I'm being a little bit rougher with her than I normally am, but I'll stop the moment she utters the word.

She never does, though, instead breaking the kiss to grab the bottom of my shirt and tug it over my head. Her fingers instantly find the scars on my chest and I struggle to breathe as she traces the rough and jagged patterns of each one. Her lips follow the path her fingers make, planting kisses on my skin. Callie knows where my scars came from, knows that some I did to myself while others my father gave me. I didn't give her every gory detail of what happened, wanting to spare her the ugliness of them.

After Callie is done kissing pretty much every inch of my chest, she reclines back and lifts her arms above her head so I can remove her shirt. I love that she trusts me enough to do this, without so much as tensing anymore. Once her shirt comes off, I unclasp her bra and my mouth promptly encloses her nipple.

She lets out this gasp mixed with a delirious plea as her fingers slide through my hair, tugging at the roots, both pulling me and pushing me closer. Her legs clamp down on my sides and she rocks her hips again, causing a throaty groan to escape my mouth. I just about lose it, right then and there.

Not being able to stand the little amount of clothing left on our bodies any longer, I pull away from her, only to yank her jeans and panties off, and then she helps me with the button of my pants so I can take them off. She's on the pill now, so I don't have to get a condom out of my pocket like I used to, which is a really good thing because a lot of times we get so caught up in the moment we'd probably forget about protection.

After I discard my boxers, I cover her body with mine. She's practically panting as she arches her hips and grabs at my ass so I can easily slide inside her, but I move almost painfully slow just to see that look on her face, the one I've seen many times, where her eyes glaze over and she gets lost, clutching onto my shoulder, stabbing at my flesh, holding onto me while she lets go. And there's nothing left to do but join her, wishing this is how things could always be.

Just her and me and nothing else.

Chapter 7

#116 Hang On.

Kayden

After the night I spent with Callie, it feels like things are going to be okay. That maybe I can let all this shit go and not worry about it. That maybe I'll never get resolution for what happened to me and that I just need to move on. I want to, but I'm not sure I can.

It's morning and I'm hanging out in my room, trying to catch up on some assignments, when my phone starts to ring. I cringe when I see Dylan's name on the screen, my mind instantly thinking the phone call is going to be bad.

I almost don't answer it, but knowing it'll drive me mad if I don't, I make myself reach for the phone

67

and press talk. Niko is hanging out at the computer desk, playing a game, so I head into the hallway to talk.

'What's up?' I ask Dylan as I shut the door behind me. I'm figuring it's a call about Tyler, so when he says, 'Dad,' it almost doesn't register in my brain.

'Huh . . .? What . . .? Did you . . .?' I'm struck speechless.

Dylan says, which is seeming to become his M.O., 'Kayden, I'm so sorry. Maybe I shouldn't be telling you this.'

I make a right toward the bathrooms, maneuvering through people, practically shoving them out of my way. 'Telling me what?' Because I seriously didn't hear anything but *Dad*.

There's the sigh again. 'I found Mom and Dad, Kayden . . . and it's bad . . . well, bad depending on how you look at it.'

I make it to the bathroom and lock myself in a stall. 'How so?' I slump against the stall door, telling myself to breathe, but my heart is taking up all the fucking space in my chest. It's like I've been kicked in the gut and slammed in the face over and over again.

I found Mom and Dad.

'Dad's in the hospital.' He pauses and I can tell he's

struggling to keep his voice balanced. 'I didn't get too much information, considering Mom is the queen of lying about shit she doesn't want to talk about.' Another pause. 'Are you okay?'

I take a deep breath. Then another. And another. 'Yeah . . .'

I found Mom and Dad.

'Kayden?'

Dad's in the hospital.

Is this my resolution?

'I have to go,' I choke then hang up the phone. My pulse is pounding, my skin damp with sweat, and I can't get air into my lungs. It's been a while since I've felt this way – this bad – but I can't help it. The thoughts going through my head . . . I'd wanted resolution, but not like this.

Or did I?

Am I that kind of a person?

To wish pain upon someone else?

Am I like my father?

The last thought is fucking horrifying. I feel like I'm about to fall again, tumble into the dark, pick up that blade and slice away until whatever's inside me bleeds out. I don't want to, but I do.

I want it.

69

Want it.
Want it.
I'm barely able to hang on.

Chapter 8

#122 Dance Like it's Your Prom.

Callie

Once upon a time, there was a girl who thought she was a princess. And really, weren't all girls supposed to be?

She grew up happy, with a loving, perhaps over-doting mother, and a father who took care of her. Her older brother wasn't too bad for the most part, as much as any older brother was. And while she didn't grow up in a castle surrounded by knolls of grassland country blossoming with flowers and trees, her simple home felt like a palace in her small town. It made her feel protected and safe from all the bad she'd heard whispers of, yet wasn't sure if it existed, since she'd never seen any of it for herself.

Yes, all was well in the princess's world. But on her twelfth birthday . . . that all changed when the bad entered *the walls of her palace. He didn't break down the place or force his way in like in the books or movies. He simply walked through the door welcomed with open arms. And he didn't have fangs or sharp teeth that would warn the princess that maybe he wasn't good but a monster. No, he was dressed in normal clothes with normal teeth and he even had a normal smile. He was simply a normal guy. At least, that was what the princess thought.*

But the princess was wrong and she soon, and very tragically, found out what the bad things were she'd only heard whispers about.

In a house full of balloons and presents, the guy trapped her in a place she'd once felt safe and broke the princess into a thousand pieces that would never fully be found again. And he didn't just break them, but stole some of them as well, keeping them somewhere no one else could see them.

After it was all over, the broken princess was no more. She simply felt like a girl who was invisible. Princesses were supposed to be happy, pretty, have lots of friends, and go to parties. Not be so broken. But the girl no longer did or felt any of those things. Her palace was now a prison. And the family that had once brought her happiness felt like nothing more than ghosts in a dark and unfamiliar world she'd been forced into.

Invisible vines grew around the home, full of thorns, making it painful to both leave and stay. Nowhere felt safe. And that was how she believed things would always be, that she would suffer from the bad all on her own for the rest of her life.

But six years later, on a warm, summer night, the girl discovered she wasn't the only one being broken by bad, scary monsters. They were everywhere, destroying walls and people – destroying one guy in particular. He wasn't just a guy, though, but the most beautiful and broken guy the girl had ever seen. She knew the moment she saw him she had to save him from the monster that stood before him with his fangs out . . .

'Whatcha doing?' Seth asks as he strolls into my room without knocking. He's dressed head to toe in black with studs on his belt and an array of leather bands on his wrists. His boots are clunky, his jacket with buckles trendy.

I'm not even sure what he's supposed to be. We just sort of wandered into this gothic store and started picking out articles of clothing that weren't in the norm for us. 'Because that's what Halloween is supposed to be about, right?' Seth had said, and I'd agreed. We'd actually taken Violet, Luke's girlfriend, to pick out her costume, although hers was a lot different from mine and honestly, the girl looked like she belonged in the store.

I glance up from my laptop. 'Writing a nontraditional fairytale for my writing portfolio.'

He peers over my shoulder and reads a few sentences on the screen. 'I have a feeling from the title that this happy introduction is going to go dark.' He pauses, looking at me. 'Are you writing a story about yourself?'

I shake my head and close the laptop, feeling self-conscious. 'No, just writing about stuff I know.'

He raises his eyebrows in skepticism. 'You know, you're brave if you tell your story.'

I set the laptop on the nightstand. 'But it's not my story. It's for a class assignment. Nothing more. Nothing less.'

'Hmmm . . .' He's not buying it, but drops it anyway, which is good because his accusation is making me the slightest bit uncomfortable. 'So you about ready for tonight?'

I nod as I cross the room and throw open the closet door. 'Yeah, should I get dressed now, though? Or take the dress with me and change somewhere else?' I grab the hanger with the dress on and step back into the room. 'I'm not sure if I should wander around dressed like this.'

Seth rolls his eyes at me. 'Oh, my darling Callie, it's Halloween. You could walk around naked and people wouldn't think too much of it.'

My cheeks start to heat. 'Well, I'm not going to do that.'

'Yeah, we can leave that to me.' He waggles his eyebrows with a teasing glint in his eyes that makes me giggle.

'Fine, I'll put the dress on now.' I step back into the closest and slip out of my pants and T-shirt. 'So what's Greyson dressed up as?'

'His normal, adorable self,' Seth answers.

'He didn't want to dress up?' I slip the dress off the hanger and hesitate, deciding if I really want to wear this. Yeah, it's just a dress, but it's shorter than the few I've worn over the last few months. It's gorgeous, though – dark blue with black lines decorated with studs that run vertically and horizontally in the chest area. To go with it, I have a pair of lacy knee-high stockings, black knee-high boots, and a velvet choker. When I bought it, I had this image of a gothic rocker chick, which is totally unlike the usual stuff I wear.

Deciding that I need to do this, I get dressed then twist my hair up, leaving a few stray waves out to frame my face. Even though my jacket doesn't really go with it, I still grab it from the hanger, knowing I'm going to freeze to death without it.

'Ta-da!' I exclaim as I spring out of the closet with my hands up, striking a pose.

Seth is messing around with his phone, and when he glances up, his jaw drops. 'Holy shit, you look hot.'

I instantly wrap my arms around myself. 'Maybe I should change.'

Shaking his head, his eyes scroll up my attire. 'No way. You are staying just like that.' He waltzes up to me, reaching into his jacket pocket. 'And I have two more things to add some detail to your hot ass.'

'Seth,' I hiss because his compliments are embarrassing me, 'stop saying that.'

When he takes his hand out, he has two items in his palm – a tube of lipstick and eyeliner. 'Well, you better get used to it because you're going to hear it a lot tonight, especially from Kayden.' He grins as he pats the desk chair. 'Now sit down and put this stuff on.'

I take the lipstick, which is a dark red, and the kohl eyeliner. 'Where did you get this stuff?'

He shrugs as he hands me my compact and then sits down on the bed. 'I borrowed it from Violet.'

I click open the compact and set it on the desk. 'Did you ask or just take it?'

'I told her what it was for,' he says, motioning at me to get a move on. 'Now would you hurry your beautiful ass up? We're going to be late.'

I lean over and begin to apply the liner. 'Violet really didn't mind that it was for me, then?'

'No, it was the least she could do after you helped her with kickboxing and costume shopping today,' he says as I apply the lipstick.

I rub my lips together as I put the cap on. 'She doesn't owe me anything, Seth. I was glad to help her.'

'I know, but she didn't mind. Besides, I think, even though she won't admit it, she likes having friends.'

'Yeah, maybe.' Although I think there's way more to it than that. When I first met Violet, I thought she was mean. And honestly, I was under the impression that she might have been a prostitute. But now, after getting to know her and seeing the stuff on the news about her parents' deaths, I think Violet has even more problems than I do.

I hand Seth back the makeup then slip my jacket on, wishing Kayden could have ridden with me instead of meeting us there, but I understand he's busy with practice and stuff.

Seth must sense some sort of weird vibe from me because he links his arm through mine and tugs me out the door. It's pretty quiet on the elevator ride down, but once we reach the bottom, all bets are off.

'So this is how the youngins celebrate Halloween, huh?' I ask, my eyes wide as I take in the lounge area packed with people dressed up in so many different types of costume it's madness I tell you. Everything from ghosts to slutty nurses to some sort of strange-looking zucchini costumes is present. There's music playing and people are chatting and laughing, and some are even running around and screaming as they drink from plastic cups I'm sure aren't filled with punch. Where their RA is, I have no clue, but I'm guessing nowhere within a mile radius, since I'm pretty sure the noise can be heard from that far.

'Wait until we get to the concert,' Seth promises, noting my shocked stare.

'I've never been to a concert,' I admit as we turn for the exit and step outside into the frigid breeze. The ground is frozen, making the heeled boots I'm wearing a little complicated to walk in. The sun has set; the moon and stars are bright in the sky and twinkling right along with all the orange, black, and purple lights around the area.

'I know you haven't.' Seth steers us to the grass covered by a thin layer of snow and we start to make our way to the parking lot. 'I promise you're going to love it, though. In fact, I think . . .' He trails off at the sight of a figure crossing the grass toward us. It takes me a moment or two longer to realize who it is.

'Hey, what are you doing there?' I ask, releasing Seth's arm and meeting Kayden halfway. 'I thought you had practice.'

He doesn't answer until he reaches me. 'I know. I left early . . . I wanted to pick you up.' He tugs at the bottom of his sleeves, seeming both nervous and excited.

I throw my arms around him and hug him tightly. 'You didn't have to do that.'

He looks amazing tonight in his black and grey plaid shirt that's unbuttoned enough so I can see the black T-shirt he's wearing that shows off his muscular abs. It's topped off with a leather jacket, black jeans, and boots, his brown hair just the slightest bit messy in the sexiest way possible. Not really a Halloween costume, but totally not his norm and makes him even more ridiculously better looking than he already is.

'I know I didn't.' He kisses my temple then pulls back to look me in the eye. 'But I wanted to.' He opens his mouth to say something else, but then his gaze drifts down my attire. I'm still holding the jacket, even though it's freezing, so he gets the full view of me.

'Holy shit,' he breathes, his arms falling to his sides. He scratches at his wrist, eyes drinking me in. 'You look—'

'Don't say hot,' Seth warns, strolling up to us. 'She seems to take that a bit offensively.'

The corners of Kayden's mouth quirk. 'I was actually going to say beautiful.'

'Liar,' Seth coughs, but then grins.

Repressing a smile, Kayden lifts one of his arms toward me. The first thing I notice is that there's something sticking out of the sleeve of his shirt . . . a piece of gauze maybe. But then my eyes travel to what's in his hand. A rose with a short, bare stem. He takes it and tucks it in my hair beside my ear, making me feel pretty. I've never been a fan of looking this way. That is, until now. But I think that has more to do with the way Kayden is looking at me, with this lustful, burning desire.

Screw prom.

This is so, so much better.

I'm about to tell him how much I love him when my attention darts to a pale figure running across the grass, yelling, 'Woo HOO! Halloween fucking rocks!'

He looks familiar and I squint to get a better look at what's going on. 'Wait. Is he . . .?' I trail off when

I realize the reason why the figure is so pale. 'He's *naked*!'

Kayden's eyes widen as he tracks my gaze then he places a hand over my eyes. 'What the hell is it with streakers and Halloween? I swear I see at least one a year.'

Seth chuckles. 'It's the freedom in the air, to be whoever you want to be.'

'I'm pretty sure he's in my English class,' I say. 'And I don't think I'll ever be able to look him in the eye again.'

'Why?' Seth asks. 'You're not the one who was seen in a very unflattering outfit. You should hold your head up high, baby girl.'

'I know, but every time I look at him, I'll picture his . . .' I bite down on my lip, unable to finish the sentence, let alone get the picture of what I just witnessed.

This time Kayden laughs and he lowers his hand from my eyes. 'You're so adorable.' Then he kisses me and I don't feel shy or ashamed. Adorable I can handle. Kayden kissing me I can handle. Seeing more naked people tonight, I'm not so sure.

The night is turning out to be amazing. The atmosphere is electric, the decor is vibrant in the most eerie way possible, and the rock-combined-orchestra music the band is playing is hauntingly poetic to the point that it gives me chills. Violet calls it Symphonic Rock.

We've been dancing for a while – Seth, Greyson, Violet, and me. Kayden and Luke are hanging out at the table. Luke seems distracted by something and Kayden keeps getting texts from someone, so they're both living in their own world. It makes me a little sad that Kayden's not out here with me, but I don't have time to wallow when Violet decides she's going to teach me to dance per Seth's suggestion.

'There's no way I can dance like her,' I tell the both of them, not because I'm afraid, but because I really don't think I can. Violet dances like a mix between a ballerina and one of those rocker chicks that can head bang in the most elegant way ever. She seriously looks like she belongs on stage with a microphone in her hand, a band of guitars and violins playing in the background.

'Sure you can,' Violet says with an encouraging smile that looks foreign on her because she hardly ever smiles. She seems in a good mood tonight, though, so I decide to play along and follow her lead.

'No, move your hips,' she instructs, putting her hand on my waist and guiding me to the rhythm. I'm not one for my personal space getting invaded, but I shake it off since we're standing in the center of a crammed crowd anyway, and try to do what she says. 'Let the music own you. Don't overthink it.'

'And dance like you mean it!' Seth shouts over the music as he raises his hands in the air.

I take a deep inhale and try to do what they both said, but I've never been one for dancing.

'You're overthinking it,' Seth tells me, his eyes wandering over my shoulders. 'And now you have the perfect distraction.' My brows furrow as he mouths, *Dance like it's your prom.*

All I can picture when he says it is what I've seen on movies. Bad music and decorations while people way too overdressed rock back and forth with their hands on each other or do some sort of silly dance-off. But then Kayden comes up to me, takes my hand, and spins me around, causing laughter to erupt from my lips.

'Aw, and the secret dance moves come out,' I say, laughing when he spins me again and then crashes me against his chest. Kayden once told me that he secretly knew how to dance because his mother used him as a dance partner when he was younger.

His arms slide around me as I rest my head on his

shoulder. 'That was supposed to be a secret,' he whispers in my ear, giving my lobe a soft nip.

The band takes a break and the DJ turns on a song I know. 'My Immortal' by Evanescence. It's slow and relaxing and I find myself unstiffening and leaning against Kayden as I rock to the music and drift away from reality.

'I hope you're having fun tonight,' he whispers in my ear, his hand on the small of my back pulling me closer. There's something in his touch – a desperation.

'Of course I am.' My eyelids slip shut as the warmth of his body drowns me and I pull him closer, wishing he knew that everything was going to be okay. If only I could make him see that somehow, that he'll always have me, that he'll never be alone.

'Good. That's all I want for you – nothing but fun.' His breath catches. 'You deserve to be happy.'

I angle my chin up to look him in the eye. 'I am happy.' *Unlike him*. He looks like he's in pain, on the verge of crying. 'Who was texting you?'

He shuts his eyes and shakes his head. 'I don't want to talk about it tonight, don't want to make another one of your nights depressing.'

Where the heck is this coming from?

'You don't make any of my nights depressing. What

the fuck, Kayden?' It's rare for me to curse, so when I do, it has a purpose. Right now, I'm panicking because he looks like a guy that's about to break up with his girlfriend. 'A-are you b-breaking up with me?'

His eyes snap wide in horror. 'What? No! Why the hell would you say that?'

'Because you look like you're about to!'

'I would never say that to you! Ever!'

We're yelling over the music and I hate it. We never yell, even behind doors, only talk passionately. But this is yelling and it's the worst feeling in the world.

As if he suddenly realizes we're in a crowded place, he lowers his voice as he takes my hand. 'Will you come with me? I have something . . .' He exhales loudly and runs his free hand through his hair. 'I have something I need to talk to you about.'

Swallowing the lump in my throat, I nod, then follow him off the dance floor, waving to Seth on my way. Seth gives me a concerned look and then puts his finger and thumb up to the side of his face like a phone. I nod, understanding he wants me to call him later. Then I turn and focus on my steps, because that's easier than focusing on what the hell just caused Kayden and me to yell at each other for the first time.

After we collect our jackets from coat check, we step

outside into the buzzing air that nips at my skin. I instantly slip my jacket on and zip it up, shivering as Kayden leads me to his car. He opens the passenger door for me without saying a word, then rounds the car and gets in and turns on the engine, cranking up the heat. He stares out the window, gripping the steering wheel so firmly his hands begin to tremble.

'I fucked up,' he finally says, pulling his hands away from the wheel and wiping his palms on his jeans.

I'm about to ask him what he messed up with, but he rolls up the sleeve of his shirt and shows me the answer. Earlier, when he'd picked me up, I thought I'd noticed a piece of gauze sticking out of his shirt, but I'd stupidly gotten sidetracked by the rose and naked man and had completely forgotten to ask him about it.

God, I should have asked him.

'What happened?' I whisper, even though I sadly know the answer.

He shuts his eyes and rubs his hand down his face, releasing a weighted breath. 'I was feeling a lot of pressure lately and instead of dealing with it, I let it eat away at me. Then some shit happened today . . . and I . . . I sort of just lost it.' He opens his eyes, but looks ahead instead of at me. 'That's why I was able to pick you up today. I had to miss practice so I could go talk to my therapist.'

I know therapy is good for him, glad he does it, but still, sometimes I wish he'd talk to me, too, about stuff.

'What was the stuff that happened today? Or do you not want to talk about it?'

He rubs his hand down his face again, this time so roughly I'm worried he's doing it to cause himself physical pain. 'I should have talked to you to begin with, instead of doing what I did. The therapist says it happens, though. Relapses happen.' He squeezes his eyes closed, a tear or two slips out. I'm not sure what to do or say, if there's anything I can do or say since I don't know what this is about. I know enough to know his cutting comes when he doesn't want to feel an emotional pain, but what caused him emotional pain?

I'm about to ask him, to try to get him to talk to me again, but this time he gives it to me without me asking. His eyes open and he looks at me, not bothering to hide the tears. 'Dylan found my mother and father.'

Chapter 9

#145 Fall in Love with the Same Person Again.

Kayden

I've always been good at pretending. I pretended that my father wasn't an abusive asshole for eighteen years of my life. That my mother wasn't a sedated zombie for the same amount of time. For twelve years, I pretended that I didn't cut myself because physical pain was easier than emotional. Pretending in front of Callie has always been hard, though. She's not so easily persuaded to believe things she knows aren't real just because it's easier to deal with than the ugly truth.

Callie always wants the truth, no matter how raw and painful it is. And I need to learn how to give it to her, which is something my therapist and I talked about today after I went in for an emergency visit.

It was Dylan's call that set me off, but it was the emotions that surfaced afterward that sent me over the edge. Anger. Hurt. Blinding rage. Relief. Guilt over the relief. It ate away at my soul and heart, and instead of feeling it, even though I fought to hang on, I slipped up and let a razor eat away at my flesh and blood. But I still felt guilty afterward for doing it. So I sought help, which is better than what I used to do. And it's helping me get through the texts Dylan's sending me of updates on what he found out.

And now I'm seeking Callie, even though I'm scared shitless to put myself out there.

'What do you mean he found them?' Callie's eyes are huge against the pale moonlight. She keeps redirecting her focus from my face to my wrist that's wrapped in gauze.

I want to touch her, but am afraid to. 'I mean, he got a hold of them.' I shrug then shrug again, my shoulders feeling as heavy as pounds of rocks. 'They're at a hospital. Been in there for a while. I guess there was some kind of accident and my father's hurt pretty bad or something.'

If it's even possible, her eyes enlarge even more. 'What exactly is wrong with him?'

'I'm not sure.' I scratch at my wrist, making the

fresh cut burn. The sensation is both soothing and frightening, a love/hate thing. 'Dylan didn't know all the details yet, probably because my mother wouldn't give them to him, but I guess he's been in the hospital for a few weeks now. Not sure why yet – what exactly's wrong with him.'

Callie put her hand over mine, probably so I'll stop scratching at my wrist. 'How do you not know all this, though? I mean, how did your brother get a hold of them?'

I swallow the lump in my throat caused by her fingers so close to the cut, a cut we both know came from my own hand. 'Tyler broke down and spilled it to Dylan. I guess he'd been with them for a while, but after the accident with my father, he took off and started hitchhiking to Dylan's house.'

'And where are your mother and father now? I mean, I know they're in a hospital, but where exactly?'

'I'm not sure. Dylan said all Tyler gave was a phone number. He said he's still trying to get all the details from my mother, but it's like pulling teeth.' I smash my lips together so tightly they go numb. 'That's how my family is, Callie. They keep secrets. From each other. From the world. No one knows who the Owens are, not even the Owens sometimes.' I'm about to start crying again, which is fucking ridiculous. I don't need to be crying over anything, do I? I don't know what to feel. All those years of being beat, both mentally and physically, are rendering me incapable of feeling the right things in this type of situation.

'I think I'm broken,' I whisper as a tear or two fall from my eyes. I feel like such a fucking pussy. This is ridiculous. Crying over something so stupid. Something I shouldn't be crying over.

Shaking her head, Callie climbs over the console and sits on my lap, facing me with a leg on each side. 'You're not broken, Kayden. Why would you ever say that?'

'Because . . .' My hands start to quiver as she guides my arms around her waist. 'Because a tiny part of me doesn't even feel bad for him.' Before I can see her reaction, which I'm sure is filled with disgust, I lower my head onto her shoulder and breathe in her comforting scent.

After a few minutes of gripping onto her and sobbing, I manage to get my crying under control, but the silence in the car is heavier than my tears. I'm not sure what to say to her, what she's thinking, feeling. God, I wish I could read her mind, see into her soul like I swear she sees into mine.

'You know that day when you beat up Caleb?' she finally asks, her voice slightly choked up.

It's not what I was expecting her to say, but I still lean back to look at her as I nod. 'Of course I remember it. It was the day I felt I finally did something for you, instead of the other way around.'

I'd lost it that day when I found out Caleb Miller, a guy who was a little bit older than me and grew up in our town, was the one who raped Callie when she was twelve. I'd wanted him to pay for it somehow, so I did the only thing I could – beat the shit out of him.

'Well, I remember when I heard about it – about what you did.' Her voice cracks. 'I hated to admit it, considering all of the bad stuff that happened afterward to you, but a part of me felt relieved, maybe even a little bit grateful.'

'But you deserved to feel that way,' I assure her. 'What he did to you was fucking horrible and sick and wrong.'

'Just like what your father did to you,' she says with pressing eyes. When I start to look away, she places her hand on my face and forces me to look at her. 'Kayden, I've heard some of the stories about the things he's done, and I'm pretty sure you've made sure not to tell me the worst of them, considering' – she glances down at my chest – 'how big some of those scars are.'

'But I don't want to be like him,' I say in a strangled whisper. 'I don't want to be full of rage and hate like him.'

'Why would you ever think you were like him? You're not in any way, shape, or form.'

'But I'm relieved because he's hurt, like he deserved it somehow. And that's something he would do – feel relief by hurting people.'

'That's different, Kayden. Way, way different. And you didn't hurt him.'

She's saying pretty much what my therapist said to me today when I went to talk to him about how I was feeling. And part of me gets why they're telling me this, but the other part of me – the one that fears turning out like my grandfather and my father – can't get over how full of hate my reaction is.

'I know, but . . .' I can't meet her gaze, my eyes on the parking lot, the stars in the sky, anywhere but at her.

'But what?' She urges me to tell her, to look at her, not to shut down like I have in the past. And I want to give her that. I really do, but I need to figure out how.

'What if I keep getting set off?' I finally dare say, forcing my attention back on her.

Her gaze swallows me up. 'I'm not sure what you mean.'

I raise my wrist. 'What if things only get worse and return to this? The last time my father was in my life, this shit owned me.'

Worry masks her face. 'But he's not in your life anymore.'

'He might be. I mean, what if the rest of my family takes him back. And Dylan . . . he wants me to come out there for a week. I think he suggested it because he thought it'd help being around him while going through this, but I don't know.' I shrug. 'I've never associated my family with helping me in anyway. Even Dylan.'

'Then don't go,' she states simply, cupping my face between her hands, making me look at her. 'You're not under any obligation to go there. You've suffered enough. And if you think this is going to be hard, then you deserve not to go. You have me, Seth, and Luke all here for you, so you're not alone in any of this. You're never, ever alone.'

I force down the massive lump welling in my throat. 'I know that, but I feel guilty that you guys have to put up with my shit. And I feel guilty for bailing on my family.'

'Well, you don't need to feel guilty about anything.' Her voice shakes with anger, startling me. 'You don't owe them anything, only yourself, so do what *you* want to do and no one else.'

'But what if . . . what if *she* calls me?'

'You mean your mom?'

'Yeah, I'm not sure I ever want to talk to her again.' I hate that I sound like a scared little boy, but I can't seem to control it. My mother was the type of woman who pretended not to see anything, even though she saw *everything*. All those years she let my father beat me, even called me in sick for school when I was too broken to go. 'Sometimes, I feel like I hate her just as much as my father.' I raise my hands between us and let my head fall into them. 'God, I don't want to do this – go back to that shit. I thought I'd moved on from it.'

'You don't have to let her into your life. If they don't make you happy, don't let them in. Life is all about the happiness, Kayden, and you should never settle for anything less.' Callie opens the driver-side door so she can climb out of the car. 'Now scoot over. I'm going to take you somewhere.'

I lift my head up to look at her. 'But what about the concert? You were looking forward to this and I can go back inside. It's probably better if I do anyway, instead of sitting out here having a pity party.'

She rolls her eyes, lightening the mood a smidgeon. 'You're not having a pity party.' She enfolds her arms around herself, shivering as her breath puffs out. 'And besides, it wasn't the concert I was looking forward to so much as spending time with you all dressed up.'

'And I want to give that to you. You deserve to have what you want.'

Her intense gaze is locked on mine. 'I have what I want every single day.'

Is it possible to fall in love with someone even when you're already in love with them? Because I'm pretty sure I just did.

'Where are we going?'

She motions me to scoot over to the passenger seat. 'No way. I'm not telling. You're just going to have to trust me.'

It only takes me a beat to move over. Because in the end, I do trust her more than anything else in my life.

Chapter 10

#146 Relive the Best Part of the Past.

Callie

He freaked me out. Not with what he said about his feeling toward his family – that's understandable – but he cut himself again and has that lost look in his eyes like he did last year when he was pushing me away. And while it's not as bad as it was, it still has me worried I might lose him to himself if he decides to go back into that dark place inside his head.

Yes, I know I could live without him if I had to, know life would have to go on, but goddammit, I don't want to live my life without Kayden. He means more to me than anyone else that's in or has ever been in my life. Whether he realizes it or not, he saved me once when I was stuck in a dark place. And I want to show him so he'll understand what he means to me, that he is important, that he's a good person, and that happiness does exist every single day when he's with me.

The first place I take him to is the campus. I know he's completely confused when I pull into the mostly vacant parking lot and park the car as close as I can to the main entrance.

'You know it's almost midnight,' Kayden says, unbuckling his seatbelt. 'If someone sees us, they might call the cops, especially considering it's Halloween.'

'I know.' I unfasten my own seatbelt, open the door, and the night breeze is gusting in. 'But it's worth the risk. I promise.'

Confused, he gets out of the car then meets me at the front and slips his fingers through mine. We walk silently across the icy grass, holding hands, and counting the stars. In the distance, I can hear the sounds of shouting and music, probably from a party, but still, the emptiness around us makes me feel at peace.

'This alone is making me feel better.' Kayden shucks off his jacket. 'Other than you look like you're freezing to death.'

'I'm fine,' I tell him, but he makes me take his jacket anyway. I slip my arms through the sleeves and breathe the musky scent of his cologne.

'Smell good?' He cracks a smile for the first time when he notices me sniffing the fabric of his jacket.

'I like the smell of you,' I admit, taking another deep inhale. His smile expands and makes my heart in my chest do the same thing. 'I'm glad you're smiling; I was getting worried.'

He sighs, the smile vanishing from his face. 'I hate that I make you worry so much.'

'You worry about me all the time,' I point out, 'and whether or not I'm getting what I deserve, which I am.'

His lips part to argue, but then he seals them back up when I come to a stop in the center of the sidewalk. The only thing nearby is the old-looking brick entrance to the main office of the University of Wyoming that's surrounded by trees and a few benches.

'So this' – I gesture at the ground with my hand – 'is the first thing I want to show you.'

His brow furrows as he stares down at the concrete. 'Okay . . . It's a really nice spot of sidewalk, I guess.' He lifts his gaze back up to me. 'I'm so confused.'

'I can tell.' I'm trying not to laugh at him, but his puzzlement is cute. 'This is where you first ran into me. Literally.'

Recognition clicks. 'Shit, I remember that. I was trying to catch a football Luke threw and totally took you out.' He shakes his head, but the rigidness in his body is starting to unravel as his mind wanders to something else. 'I can't believe you ever went out with me after that.'

'I didn't want to,' I admit. 'Or I was afraid of you anyway.'

'I don't blame you. I'm surprised you didn't get hurt.'

'No, I wasn't afraid of you because of that.'

'What do you mean?' he wonders, getting confused all over again. 'Why were you afraid of me, then?'

I tug on his arm, pulling him in the direction of the car. 'Come on and I'll show you.'

'Okay, I know this restaurant,' he says proudly after the waitress seats us in a corner booth that's decorated with a glowing pumpkin and a purple and black lantern. It's late enough that there's hardly anyone around, except for a few drunk college kids in the bar area dressed up for Halloween. 'This is where we first had dinner. But it wasn't a date. Luke and Seth were here.'

'I remember.' I'm all smiles as I open my menu. 'But it was the closest thing I had to a date.'

'Callie, I'm sorry' – he frowns – 'that you were so alone for so long.'

'I didn't bring you here to feel sorry for me, Kayden.'

I glance up from the menu and meet his gaze. 'Me being alone was based on the fact that I didn't trust anyone. But that night, I trusted you.'

'Really?' he asks doubtfully as he flips open the menu in front of him. 'You seemed like you didn't want to have anything to do with me, especially when I reached out to take your hand.'

'That's because I was terrified. I had to run to the bathroom to empty out my stomach,' I explain. When he starts to say something, I add, 'I didn't bring you here to talk about my past problems. I've done enough of that to last me a lifetime.' I reach across the table and place my hand over his. 'I brought you here to show you this.' I nod at my hand on his. 'This is possible because of you.'

He shakes his head. 'No, this is possible because you're strong. You're the strongest person I've ever met, Callie. I swear to God, I don't know how you do it.'

'I do it because I have good people in my life that make everything worth it.'

He sighs, disheartened. 'You're always glowing with positivity. I wish I could be like that.'

'Yeah, *now* I am. But if you had talked to me before college, you wouldn't have thought so. I was weak back then.'

His hand begins to tremble beneath mine. 'That's not true. Remember that night . . . that night you stepped in when,' he lowers his voice, 'when my father was beating me. It takes a shitload of strength to do that.'

'And it takes a shitload of strength to survive that,' I press, giving his hand a gentle squeeze. 'And to tell someone about it. Like you did.'

He grits his teeth. 'Eventually, but I put you through hell until I did.'

'It took me forever with Caleb.' My pressing tone meets his. 'It took me almost seven years to tell anyone. And you didn't put me through hell.'

He doesn't know what to say. Kayden has always been great at trying to give me confidence, but being on the receiving end of the line has always been a struggle for him. In high school, I would have never believed it. Gorgeous star quarterback dating the most popular girl in school, I thought he radiated self-worth. Boy, was I wrong.

'I wish things could have been different for you,' he utters softly, tracing my knuckles with his thumb. 'I wish you could have been happy all of your life.'

'Yeah, it would have been nice,' I agree. 'I know it might sound crazy – and trust me, I wish more than anything I never knew Caleb – but the thing is, what happened to me did happen and I can't change it, so there's no use letting it ruin my life. I don't need to give Caleb that kind of power over me anymore. And besides, I might not be here with you if my life took another path, so I can look at the bad as something I had to go through to get to the good. You are my good, no matter what you want to believe. I'm sitting here, happier than I've ever been, because of you. You are my happiness.'

His gaze is flickering from my eyes to my mouth . . . from my eyes to my mouth . . . eyes . . . mouth. 'Can I kiss you right now?' he whispers when he's solely fixated on my lips. 'I really need to kiss you.'

I nod eagerly. 'Yes, please.'

He leans over the table and I meet him halfway, smashing my lips to his and willingly sinking into a passionate kiss right there in public. We don't come up for air until the waitress interrupts us to take our orders. Once she's gone, Kayden stares at me from across the table with a contemplative look on his face.

'What?' I touch my face self-consciously. 'Do I have something on my face? I am, after all, wearing enough lipstick to paint a clown's face.'

He shakes his head. 'It's nothing.' He extends his

hand toward me and rests it on the side of my face. 'Listening to you talk, the things you say, the way you look at life; you always make me feel better when I'm down. You're amazing.'

'So are you.' I relax into his touch. 'We make the perfect couple.'

He swallows hard and I think he's going to go back to his self-doubt about his worth, so he shocks me when he says, 'I think I want to . . . I want to live with you . . . You and me together.' He pauses then shakes his head determinedly. 'No. Scratch that. I *know* I do.'

My heart pitter-patters inside my chest. I don't want to get too excited, but I am. 'Are you sure? Because I don't want you to feel pressured or anything. I can wait.'

The corners of his mouth tip upward, his expression full of warmth. 'I've never been more positive about anything in my life than I am about you. I don't ever want to lose you . . . I just want to make sure you're happy.'

'I am happy. I promise.'

'And I want to move in with you. I promise.'

Unable to control my excitement any longer, I grin like a big goof. He grins back at me, a genuine smile, too. And we remain that way, smiling like two silly, lovestruck college kids until the waitress strolls up with our drinks and food and gives us a questioning look, probably thinking the goofy, elated expressions we have are because we're high.

After she sets our plates and drinks down in front of us, Kayden scoops up his burger and takes a large bite. 'So is this our last stop for the night? Or is there more?'

I pick up a handful of fries. 'What do you think?'

'I think that considering the path you're following, there's still more.' He opens his mouth and takes another massive bite of his burger, appearing so much more relaxed than he did twenty minutes ago. It makes me want to keep going down this path.

'So, if you had to guess the next place, where do you think it would be?' I pluck the onion off my burger as I wait for his answer, wondering if he's cracked the code of my path.

'You think I don't know,' he says amusedly, 'but I do.'

I shrug, equally amused. 'I'm curious if you remember.'

His brow arches. 'And what do I win if I get it right?'

'Whatever you want,' I tease, then take a bite of my burger.

He seems pleased, a big grin plastered on his face. 'Prepare to lose, then.' He reaches across the table to wipe some mayo off my lip. 'Races, spray paint, and green footprints.'

He doesn't have to say exactly where it is – we both know what those words mean. Such a simple night, at least to an outsider's point of view, but to me it was one of the most magical, life-changing nights of my life.

Chapter 11

#149 Channel Your Inner Daredevil.

Callie

Thirty minutes later, we're entering a store we went to right before we tagged a rock at a very famous tagging area, and right after Kayden and I first danced over a year ago. I was a little buzzed that night and felt so free hanging out with Kayden, Seth, and Luke because it was the first time I felt like I had friends.

The store is still the same, a little rundown and sells cheap stuff for cheap prices. We instantly make our way to the aisle where I once stepped on a can of green spray paint and got it all over the floor. It was during a sort of wrestling match between Kayden and I after Luke had turned the night into a game.

'Holy shit. I can't believe you can still see it,' Kayden

says as we both stare at the faint green shoeprint staining the dingy linoleum floor.

I slap my hand over my mouth as a giggle escapes. 'I should feel bad, right?'

Kayden shakes his head as I move my foot over the print – the perfect fit. 'No way. If anything, you should feel proud. You marked that night forever.'

'Well, as long as this store exists, but it was definitely a night to be marked.' I pause and then decide to admit the truth. 'You know, when we were in the cab by ourselves, I kind of wanted you to kiss me. Although, I probably would have freaked out, so maybe it's a good thing you didn't. I don't think I was quite ready for it yet.'

As he processes my words, he steps toward me, our bodies just inches away from one another. 'I wanted to kiss you that night, but was afraid.'

I inch toward him, stealing what little space there is remaining between us. 'Of what?'

'That I would like it, that it would be wrong because I had a girlfriend, that I wasn't good enough for you.' He wets his lips with his tongue, his attention fixed on my lips. 'Should we have a do-over?'

I nod enthusiastically and without any hesitation, his mouth collides with mine so forcefully I wonder if the impact will leave a bruise. But I don't care. Let me bruise. All I can concentrate on now is his tongue parting my lips as he consumes me. The force sends me backward and I slam into the shelf behind me, another bruise perhaps, but again, it doesn't matter. I don't plan on breaking this kiss for anything.

But the shelf is lined with cans of spray paint and when we ram into it, a row of them tip over and fall onto the floor, making a lot of noise.

I sputter a laugh as we break the kiss and stare down at the mess we just made. 'Holy crap,' I say. 'We're cursed.'

'No way,' he breathes, his palms splayed on my back beneath my shirt. 'It's destiny, letting us have a second chance at the night I should have kissed you.'

His words sweep me away from reality and I grab the front of his shirt to pull him in for another kiss. Right as our lips reunite, someone yells, 'What the hell is going on?'

Our heads snap in the direction the voice came from. At the end of the aisle, the clerk is there, red-faced and angry as he stares at the mess we just made. He's about thirty or so, with shoulder-length hair, and wearing a name tag on his tie-dye shirt that says *Ed*.

'We'll clean it up,' I say, but Ed comes storming toward us.

'I'm so sick of you little shits coming in here and thinking it's funny to trash my store.' As Ed strides toward us, he presses his finger to his chest as he repeats, '*My* store. Not yours. Mine. I'm going to make you pay for every damn one of those spray-paint cans.'

I'm not sure what to do. The guy has this creepy look on his face like he's out of his mind and it's frightening but funny at the same time. A nervous laugh leaves my lips as Kayden grabs my hand and tugs me with him as he takes off in the other direction.

The clerk shouts at us to, 'Get your punk asses back here now!' but that only makes us move faster and laugh harder.

We don't stop until we're safely in the car and driving down the road toward the mountains, the headlights of Kayden's car lighting the way. I'm still the driver, despite Kayden's protests, because I want to be the one taking him on this journey.

'So where are you taking me now?' he asks as we head up toward the foothills.

'You don't know?' I ask, wondering if he's serious. Considering the direction we're going in, it has to be obvious. And besides, we've had a few good moments up at this place, which makes it a super important part of our past.

He glances at me with a devious look on his face as he lifts his hand. 'Actually, I do.' In his hand is a can of spray paint, which means he knew where we were going before we even got in the car. I'd be happy about this, and I am, except . . . 'Did you shoplift that can of paint?'

'The guy was a stoned asshole; I couldn't very well pay for it with him about ready to attack us,' he says, and when I sigh, he laughs. 'Relax, Callie. I threw a few bucks down on the floor before we left.' He draws a line down my cheekbone with his fingertip, eliciting an eye flutter from me. 'I know you're too nice to condone shoplifting.'

'Hey, I can be a rebel,' I say, half joking, half serious. 'I've drank underage.'

He chuckles at my lame statement. 'You're so adorable.'

Gripping onto the wheel with one hand, I aim a finger at him. 'Hey, mister, I am not always adorable. And I'm going to prove it to you.' *I am?*

That gets him to smile, which makes me smile, too, even though I have no clue how to back up my words.

Still, I rack my brain for a way to show him the daredevil side of me that I'm not sure I've discovered yet.

The idea only comes to me when I pull up to the parking spot at the bottom of the hill. I remember Seth always making jokes about how people would come up here and have sex. I used to blush like crazy when he'd joke about it and then told me Greyson and him came up here once.

I'm not even sure I can go through with it. Yeah, I'm a different person than I used to be. Much stronger and blush less. Plus, there's no one else up here tonight, so we've got the whole place to ourselves.

'What's going on in that beautiful head of yours?' Kayden asks, interrupting my dazedness.

I tear my attention from the trees in front of the car and turn in my seat to face him. The headlights are still on and between that and the moonlight I can make out his firm jawline, soft lips, and wonderfully familiar eyes.

'Callie.' He starts to squirm under the weight of my gaze. 'What's going on? Is something wrong?'

Shaking my head, I swallow my nerves and click the headlights off. We're smothered by darkness, which makes it easier to do what I'm about to. Or maybe it's the costume making me feel like someone else, someone who can take risks, be a daredevil. I really don't care where the feeling's coming from; I just do what Seth's always saying and roll with it, leaning over the console and kissing Kayden without any warning. He sucks in a sharp breath as my lips brush his and then he laughs softly when my tongue sweeps across his lip, signaling that I want him to open up.

'I feel like you're about ready to show me just how unadorable you are,' he says in this low, husky voice that sends a thrill through me.

'You're completely right,' I tell him as I tug off my boots then climb over the console and onto his lap. I put a knee on each side of him then crash my lips against his. This time he opens right up, sucking my tongue into his mouth and kissing me back with equal intensity. He nips at my bottom lip as he wraps his fingers around the back of my head and guides me closer, until there's no room left between our bodies.

We've started to fog up the windows as I start to unbutton his shirt, but he catches my hand in his. 'Callie, wait. We don't have to do this,' he pants against my lips, sounding as if stopping is the last thing he wants to do. 'I didn't mean to upset you with the adorable comment.'

'You didn't upset me. I promise.' And it's the truth.

113

Right now, my mind is moving a million miles an hour, my body totally running on some sort of adrenaline high and I want to keep going, keep doing new things with Kayden, make every moment count, just like I'm always saying.

Before he can work up another protest, I slip my hand from his hold and flick another button loose on his shirt. I continue my way down it until I've got them all undone, then he slips the plaid shirt off and chucks it on the backseat. I'm about to reach for the hem of the T-shirt he's wearing to take that off, too, when he leans toward the passenger side and turns the key so the battery clicks on and heat blasts from the vents.

'Trust me. You don't want it being freezing in here. It might do weird things to my man parts,' he jokes and then peels his T-shirt off while I giggle at his comment. He's laughing as he reaches for the zipper of the jacket I have on and yanks it down. After he gets it off, he tugs the straps of my dress down enough that my bra is exposed. Then he jerks down the front of that, too, so my breasts hit the air.

Before I can even react to the somewhat still chilly air, his mouth is on me, sucking and nipping and driving my body mad. It's amazing how, even after a year, he still makes me feel the same overwhelming excitement and vulnerability I felt the first time we were together. It never gets old, whether we're in his bed or in the crammed seat of a car.

My head tips back as he continues to devour me with his mouth, moving back and forth between my breasts, only stopping when I'm on the verge of passing out from lack of oxygen. Then he undoes the button of his jeans and before I can even ask what he's doing, he reaches up the bottom of my dress. I decide to help him out and lift my hips up, snorting a laugh when I bump my head on the roof. But all humor fades when he slides the edge of my panties aside and thrusts himself inside me.

It's either the angle of my hips or the way my legs are bent, but he sinks in deep and I swear to God every one of my nerve endings explode as I gasp, clutching onto the back of the seat. It's intense. No, beyond intense, to the point where I don't think I can breathe.

'Jesus,' Kayden utters in a hoarse whisper as he grips at my waist from underneath my dress. 'This feels . . .'

'Amazing,' I finish for him, then start rocking my hips, unable to hold still a second longer.

We move rhythmically, completely in sync with each

other, like we were made for each other, which, in my opinion, we are. There is no one else in the world that will make me feel the way Kayden does. I will never trust anyone more. Never want to be with anyone as much. He's it for me and I just hope that it's the same way for him. That he wants to move in with me like he said. Be with me, maybe forever.

Chapter 12

#150 Rewrite Beautiful Words in Your Own Beautiful Way.

Kayden

'That was . . .' I can barely breathe, let alone finish the sentence. Not after that. Sex in a car with Callie. How the hell did a really shitty night turn into something so amazing? I'd been so upset about all the stuff with my dad and how it was making me feel so ugly inside. Plus, I'd had a relapse. I felt like I was sinking toward the bottom of despair and now I feel like I'm on cloud nine running on fucking rainbows. But I don't think it's just the sex; it's the memories that are doing it to me, too. Through all of the craziness and crappiness that's happened, I'd somehow lost sight of all the good stuff that has happened and is still happening.

'I must be good if I'm making you speechless.' She tries to be playful, but even through the dark I can still tell that she's blushing by the way she turns her head and lets strands of hair fall into her face.

'You're perfect.' I taste her lips one more time before I help her put her bra back into place, then the straps of her dress. She shivers as my fingers brush her shoulders and it makes me smile that my touch still does this to her after almost a year. 'You always are.'

She smiles as she hops back into the driver's seat so I can put my shirt back on. 'I feel like I'm high,' she admits as she puts my jacket back on.

'So you like being naughty,' I tease as I button up my shirt.

Slipping her foot into her boot, she shrugs, but her lips threaten to turn upward. 'Maybe.'

I want to tell her she's adorable, but that's kind of what started this whole thing to begin with. Okay, maybe I should call her it again. Hell, I need to start calling her it a lot more.

Before I can say anything else, though, she pushes open the door to get out. 'Are you ready to visit the next place?' she asks, wiggling her other foot into her boot before she swings her feet out onto the ground.

I nod, grabbing the can of spray paint from the

center console before I hop out of the car with her. I take her hand as soon as we reach the path, unable to keep myself from touching her. That's the thing with Callie – something as simple as her touch can warm the cold inside me. Her words are so much more powerful. They not only warm the cold, but melt it into a puddle.

It's what her words did for me at the restaurant. It's why I told her I want to move in with her. I think I always have, but wasn't able to say it until that moment when I realized not only how much she meant to me, but how much I meant to her. I may fight it, may worry I'm not good enough for her, but in the end, I'm what she seems to want and she deserves to have what she wants, so I'm giving it to her – giving me to her the best I can.

'We probably should have brought flashlights,' Callie says as the path starts to wind into the hills, making the city lights below disappear and our surroundings shadow over.

I reach into my pocket to get my phone and swipe my finger across the screen so it lights up. 'How about this?' I hold it up and aim it down on the path.

'You're brilliant,' she says then picks up the pace, pretty much skipping through the dark.

'Careful.' I grip onto her as she starts to slip on a patch of ice.

She keeps skipping and I end up shuffling after her until we reach the steep rock I once sat on with her before we even kissed. There's a light layer of snow on some of the rocks and icy spots on the ground.

'I'm not sure we should climb up that in the dark,' I tell her, pulling her toward me until her back is pressed against my chest.

'But we climbed them in the dark before with Seth and Luke,' she says as I circle my arms around her waist.

'I know, but I love you now and would die if anything happened to you.' I kiss the sensitive spot behind her ear and she sighs.

'All right, you win, but only because you made such a beautiful argument.' She takes a seat on a small rock and faces the path we just walked up. 'Remember how each time we came up here, you had to help me climb up the rocks?'

I nod and sit beside her, turning the timer on my screen on so it's at the max – we have ten minutes of light. 'I also remember how I had a naughty dream about you where I was helping you down the rocks.' I set the phone down beside my feet and try to get comfortable even though the ground is freezing my ass.

Her head snaps in my direction. 'What? When?'

'The night we first came here.'

'But you were still dating Daisy then?'

'It didn't mean I wasn't attracted to you,' I tell her. 'Trust me, I was. Way, way attracted to you.'

She presses her lips together as if she wants to say something, but is fighting it.

'What's on your mind?' I brush my finger across the inside of her wrist.

Her shoulders rise and fall as she heavy-heartedly shrugs. 'You know, I never got how you were attracted to me when you were dating her. I mean, I know you love me now, but it never made sense why you'd break up with her then want to date me right after. I mean, I know she was a bitch, but she was . . . well, she was really, really pretty.' A thousand protests run through my mind, but before I can say anything she adds, 'I'm not saying that so you'll compliment me. I know you love me now. I was just telling you how I felt in the past, since this is a night about the past.'

It takes me a moment to find my voice, but only because I'm still shocked about the first thing she said. 'First of all, let's get something straight. All looks aside, you are a thousand times a better person than Daisy will ever be. The girl was more than a bitch. She was evil and self-centered. She never asked about my scars, never tried to get to know me in the way you did, when I felt completely and utterly vulnerable, but in a way I needed to be. You saved me, Callie, not only from my father, but from myself and a life full of misery and self-loathing. And yeah, I know I still have a ways to go, but you still help me even now.'

'Good, I'm glad. I love helping—'

I cover her mouth with my hand, silencing her. 'I'm not done yet.' I position my hands so her face is trapped between them, wishing it wasn't so dark so I could see my favorite part about her – her eyes. They're a mirror to her emotions and I love being able to see what she's feeling whenever I look into them. 'And second of all, you're a million times more beautiful than Daisy will ever be.' She starts to protest, but I talk over her. 'And not just because you're beautiful on the inside, which I know you're about ready to say, but because you are ridiculously beautiful in a way that almost seems unreal sometimes.'

'Kayden, I appreciate you saying that, but I know I'm not,' she says. 'I know what I am, though, which is average, and I'm okay with that.'

'You'll never be average, Callie.' I wish she'd get the full extent of what I'm trying to say. 'Daisy was like plastic, all fake nails and tan, bleached hair, and fancy clothes – nothing about her was real. You' – I bring her lips closer to mine – 'you're real. Everything from your freckles, to those beautiful, gorgeous eyes of yours, to those fucking perfect lips. You're unconventionally beautiful, the kind of beautiful people can't even understand because it's not generic and created – it just is.'

She's quiet for what feels like an eternity, the soft sound of her breathing filling the silence between us. 'You're turning into quite the master of words,' she says softly. 'You just put this writer to shame.'

My lips tug upward, but I'm not ready to smile just yet. 'But you get what I'm saying, right? You understand how beautiful you are inside and out?'

She nods and I feel her cheeks move as she smiles. 'But only if you understand just how much I need you and how much I deserve you.'

It takes a lot for me to say it, but I know I have to – know it's right for the moment. 'All right, it's a deal,' I say, then lean in to kiss her, taking my time, savoring the feel of her lips.

I pull away about eight minutes later when the screen

clicks off and darkness surrounds us. Picking it up, I reset it for another ten minutes then take the spray can out of my pocket. 'So, what are you planning on putting on the rock this time?' I ask, giving the can to her.

'Hmmm . . .' She taps her finger against her lip then hands the can back to me. 'I think you should be the one to do it.'

'No way. You're the writer.'

She gets to her feet and brushes the dirt and little bits of snow off her ass. 'Nope. I'm giving you the honors tonight, since you've been on a roll with beautiful words.' When I don't get up right away, she offers her hand to me. 'Come on, Kayden. After what you just said to me, this should be a piece of cake.'

I thread my fingers through hers and get to my feet, giving the can a little shake. Then I stare at the rock. And stare at the rock. And stare. And stare. And stare.

'It's like when I look at my computer screen sometimes.' She playfully pokes me in the side. 'Only instead of a cursor doing the tormenting it's a can of paint.'

I lift the can to write something, but the pressure is getting to me. My mind is blank until suddenly I get an idea as I remember the night we came up here the first time. Callie had painted her own quote on the wall . . . that amazing quote.

Smiling, I press the nozzle and move my hand across the rock. She grabs the phone and aims it so I can see better, and so she can read what I'm writing. When I'm done, I stand back beside her and she reads it aloud.

'*In the existence of our lives, there are many coincidences that bring people together, but there's only one person that will own your heart forever,*' she reads aloud and I swear she almost cries near the end.

'Someone really smart once wrote that, I think,' I say as I put the lid back on.

'She didn't say that exactly.' She turns to face me. 'And I like your version a lot better.'

'Good.' I take her hand and hold onto to it for a thousand different reasons – to touch her, to feel comforted, to keep on standing, living, breathing. It's crazy how the night went from shitty to one of the best nights I've had in a long time. It makes me realize how much I need her and how much I need to keep working on being the guy she deserves. 'Because I mean it – all of it.'

Chapter 13

#153 Help Someone Even When They Don't Necessarily Ask For Help.

Callie

The next few weeks go by in a blur of fall leaves, midterms, and football games. Before I know it, Thanksgiving is approaching. Kayden and I haven't gotten a place of our own yet, nor have we really talked about it since that night. However, he does seem to be doing a lot better after we spent time reliving some of our past moments, and that's really all that matters, right?

I also haven't noticed any fresh cuts on his skin and he hasn't gotten upset over anything with his family, so things are going pretty smoothly. Then again, I don't think much has happened other than Dylan calling to check in and to see if Kayden is planning on going out there for Thanksgiving break.

'So have you decided what you're going to do yet?' I ask Kayden. He stopped by my dorm after football practice when I was in the middle of folding my laundry. There are piles of clothes on the bed and I'm still working on the pile in the basket. By the time I get finished, there'll probably be more to clean and fold.

Kayden is lying on the floor, since there's no room anywhere else, throwing a football up in the air and catching it. 'About Thanksgiving?'

I nod, folding a shirt and adding it to a stack near the foot of the bed. 'I was just wondering if you decided whether you're going to go to Virginia or not.' It's a sensitive subject, so I keep my voice light.

He tosses the football in the air and catches it before he responds. 'What do you think I should do?' he asks, tipping his head back to look at me.

I grab a pair of jeans from the basket. 'Kayden, I don't really think I should make that choice for you.'

'Yeah, I guess I worded that wrong.' He sets the football down and rolls to his side so he can easily look at me. 'I just meant . . . I mean, what are you doing?'

'For Thanksgiving?' I shrug as I fold the jeans. 'Going

home. You know how my mom is with holidays. She'd be super upset if I didn't come home. You can come with me, though, if you don't want to go to Virginia.'

He bobs his head up and down, contemplating something. 'Yeah, I don't think I'm up for going back home really.' He seems guilty about it, which he shouldn't be.

'You don't have to think of it as going home. Just visiting my family for Thanksgiving.'

'Yeah, but not thinking of it as home is part of the problem because it never really was.' He flips on his stomach and pushes himself up to his feet, his grey T-shirt riding up just enough for me to see a little bit of his firm stomach. 'And, I think I want to find some sort of place that I can call home.' He wavers. 'So I think maybe I should go to Virginia and try out this whole holiday thing with Dylan. I mean, he hasn't brought up anything about my mom or dad lately, so I should be okay. I think, maybe it's a good idea. And besides, I think it's time I tried to handle that stuff.' He glances at the healing scar on his wrist. 'So that I don't slip up again.'

I feel a ping of sadness in my stomach at the idea of spending a week away from him. Plus, there'd be almost a country's worth of distance between us. Yet,

I know those are both selfish reasons and in the end, it would be really nice for him to be able to get along with Dylan, especially if he wants to.

'If you feel like you should go to Virginia, then you should go to Virginia.' I collect a stack of jeans to put in the dresser. 'It'd be good for you to get to know Dylan and maybe even Tyler if he's going to be there and you think you want to see him.'

'He's still in rehab.' He scoops up the football from the floor as I open the drawer and put the clothes in. 'But I might get to see him. I think, anyway.'

'Good.' Mustering up my best smile, I turn to face him. I am happy for him and everything, but I just hope it goes well for him. I worry. 'I'll miss you, though.'

'You could always come with me,' he says with hope as he clutches onto the football.

'I wish I could, but I already told my mom I'd come home. Plus, Jackson's going to be there and I haven't seen him since Spring Break. And I made a number on the list to try to have a better relationship with him.' I point at my door where the whiteboard with the to-do list usually is, but furrow my brow when I realize it's gone.

'What on earth? Where's my list?' I glance at Kayden. 'Was it here when you came over today?'

He shrugs, rotating the football in his hand. 'I have no idea.'

I scratch my head. 'Maybe Seth took it for some reason.' I start to reach for my phone. 'I should call him and ask.'

'But anyway,' Kayden says, clearly cutting me off, 'that's good you're trying to patch things up with your brother.' He grabs my hand as I give him a questioning look. 'I know that's been hard for you, considering Caleb was his best friend.'

I decide to ignore his weird sidetracking thing – for now anyway – but I will get to the bottom of it.

'He's been really nice since I finally told him what happened,' I say as Kayden gives my arm a tug and lures me toward him. 'I don't want to be mad at him anymore. It was too exhausting and there's no point in holding grudges.'

The corner of his lips tip to a half-smile. 'You always say stuff that I feel applies to me.'

'Oh, that's not what I meant,' I begin to protest as our bodies greet each other. 'What happened between Jackson and me isn't the same as what your father and mother did to you. At all.' I feel horrible for what I said. Kayden should be able to hold a grudge against his father and mother, forever in my opinion. After his father stabbed him and nearly killed him – stuff like that just doesn't erase. The large scar on Kayden's side proves that.

'Callie, relax. I know you weren't referring to me.' He gently tugs on a loose strand of my hair. 'I was just teasing you.'

I assess him carefully. He seems like he's being honest and looks almost happy. 'You seem in a good mood. What's up?'

He rolls his tongue in his mouth to keep from smiling. 'It's nothing. I'm just happy I'm here with you.'

I tip my head and study him suspiciously. 'No, something's up. You're like super happy and you just purposely sidetracked me from the fact that the list is missing from the door.'

'Okay, maybe there is something on.' He's so cute, trying to restrain a grin. 'But I can't tell you right now.'

'Is it bad?'

'No. It's good, I think.' He's totally enjoying this.

'Okay, now I really want to know.' I pout out my lip. 'Please.'

Chuckling under his breath, he reaches up and touches my bottom lip with his fingertip. 'That trick's not going to work on me.'

'What trick?' I ask innocently.

He gives me a look. 'Are you trying to tell me that you don't purposefully pout your lip out when you're trying to get your way?' he asks and I get a guilty look on my face. 'Yeah, see. I can read you just as well as you can read me.' He winks at me then pulls me in for a kiss, dropping the football to the floor. Our tongues instantly tangle and within seconds he's picking me up and carrying me toward the bed.

I have every intention of pulling off his clothes and re-experiencing the moment we shared in the car a few weeks ago, but then the door swings open and Harper comes walking in.

'Oh shit.' She halts in the doorway when she spots us on the bed, legs entwined, bodies pressed together, hands all over each other – thankfully no one's clothes have come off.

'Sorry,' I apologize, sitting up while Kayden remains lying down, his fingers sketching up and down my back. 'We were just . . .' How am I supposed to finish that sentence? *We were just about to have hot, sweaty sex?* Yeah, that sentence is not coming out of my mouth.

Harper dithers in the doorway, hugging her books to her chest. 'I can come back.'

I shake my head and hop off my bed. 'No, it's okay.

I needed to run to the store anyway.' I reach for my jacket as Kayden begrudgingly gets off the bed and picks up his football.

'Hey, could you by chance pick up a roll of tape for me?' Harper asks as she drops her books onto the bed. 'I ran out last night.'

I nod. 'Sure.'

'Thanks.' She forces a smile as she starts to unbutton her jacket. 'Actually, Callie, before you leave . . . could I talk to you?' She flicks the last button undone then sets her coat on the bedpost, her eyes flicking to Kayden before they land on me. 'Alone maybe?'

'Um, yeah, sure.' I turn to Kayden who shoots me a puzzled look. 'Can I meet you out in the car?'

He nods warily. 'Sure.' He softly kisses my forehead then glances at Harper before walking out the door. Once it clicks shut, I face Harper. 'So what's up?'

'It's nothing really.' But her expression suggests otherwise as she sinks down on the bed, her shoulders slumped. 'Honestly, I don't know how to bring it up without you getting mad.'

'I won't get mad.' I don't know what else to say, since I don't know where this is going.

Sighing, she fiddles with a strand of her hair, twisting it around her finger. 'The other day I overheard you and Seth talk about stuff.' She's staring at her hair, completely fixated on it. 'About something that happened to you.'

'I'm not sure what you mean.' I sit down on my bed so we're facing each other. 'Seth and I have said a lot of things,' I tell her and then try to make a joke because she looks so sad. 'Particularly Seth. He *loves* to talk.'

A tiny smile rises on her lips, but her eyes still seem filled with sadness as she looks up at me. 'Well, it was the other day. I think you guys thought I had my headphones on and was listening to music, but I was actually trying to find something to listen to so I heard a little bit of your conversation . . . about a guy doing stuff to you.' She winces as she says it, and even though I'm used to talking about this aloud, I still wince myself.

'Yeah . . .' Again, I'm unsure of what to say.

'Sorry,' she says quickly. 'I'm sure you're wondering why I'm saying this and the truth is . . . well, the truth is I heard you say something about how you were feeling a lot better and that you have been since you talked to your parents about it. I was kind of wondering' – her gaze drops to the space on the floor between our feet – 'how you went about that.'

'Telling my parents that I was . . . raped?' It's still

so hard to say aloud, even though I've been openly talking about it for a while.

Again, she winces. 'Yeah . . . that.' She looks up at me and although she doesn't say anything about it, I think I suddenly understand why she's bringing this up. I know that pained look she's trying to keep trapped inside her because I did the same thing for years.

I'm not sure if I should ask her yet if she was raped. Stuff like this can be tricky – getting someone to tell the truth can be tricky. I should know since it took me almost seven years of carrying around this dark heaviness inside me, afraid to let it out because I was afraid of what people would think of me and honestly, I was afraid of Caleb, too.

'You don't have to tell me if you don't want to.' Harper's words rush out of her. Right now, she seems like a completely different person, but that's because she's vulnerable and scared.

'No, it's okay.' I lift my shoulders to build up some confidence. 'When it came to telling my parents, I just sort of sat them down and told them. There's really not a right or easy way to do it, other than to do it. I do think that getting to the point where you decide you're going to tell someone is the hardest part, though.'

'Did you struggle with it?' she asks. 'I mean, with getting up the courage to tell someone.'

I suck in a gradual inhale through my nose to keep the emotions inside me so I won't freak her out. 'Yeah, it took me almost seven years.'

Her eyes snap wide. 'How old were you when it happened?'

'Twelve.'

'Jesus, Callie, that's horrible.'

'Yeah, it was, but I'm trying to move on.' I pause, wondering if it's the right time to ask her something yet, but then I realize that there might not be a right time and I just have to do it. 'How old were you?'

She sighs, her shoulders slumping. 'Is it that obvious why I'm asking all this?'

'It might not be for someone else, but you have this look on your face right now that I'm kind of familiar with.'

'And what look is that?'

'Fear . . . pain.'

We exchange a look of understanding. I've always known that what happened to me has happened to other people, but I've never really discussed it with anyone who's had to live through the hellish experience.

136

'I feel those things,' she says quietly, her eyes getting watery. 'I hate that I do, though. Everyone thinks I'm so happy because that's what I show them, but I'm not as happy as I seem.'

'Everyone thought I was crazy,' I tell her. 'But I did chop off my hair with a pair of scissors and stop talking to people.'

She offers me a sympathetic look. 'Callie, that's so sad.'

'And so is pretending to be happy all the time,' I say. 'Everyone should feel okay enough to be themselves.'

She nods, agreeing. 'Yeah, but my story's not as sad as yours. I was fourteen and older.'

'That doesn't make it any better.' I stand up from the bed and cross the room to sit down beside her, my legs feeling the slightest bit wobbly. 'Rape is a horrible thing no matter what and you should tell someone about it.'

'I'm not sure if I can tell my mom.' She frowns and it makes me wonder if perhaps it was somebody living under the same roof as her.

'How about a brother or sister, then?' I suggest.

She shakes her head. 'I don't have any.'

'How about your dad?'

Her expression hardens as she grinds her teeth and balls her hands into fists. 'I'm not telling my stepfather.'

Okay, I'm pretty sure that's probably who did it to her, but I don't want to push her, or make assumptions because I can tell she's on the verge of cracking and I could be wrong. 'What about another relative or a therapist?'

She considers what I said for quite a few minutes. 'You've talked to a therapist, right? I mean, I thought I heard Seth and you talking about it at the beginning of the school year.'

'Yeah, I used to up until a couple of months ago. I can give you her number. She's really nice and understanding and gets things like this.'

'Okay, yeah, can I have her number?'

Nodding, I retrieve my phone from my pocket and text Harper the contact information of my therapist. 'You should call her today, too, while you're in this place where you can talk about it.'

'But I didn't really talk about it,' she says with a discouraged sigh. 'Not really.'

'That's not true.' I tuck my phone away. 'What you said today was a big, huge step.'

Her lips turn upward and it looks as though she might be showing me a glimpse of her real smile. I realize right there and then I've never seen it before.

'Well, I'll call her, but we'll see how it goes when it comes time to go there,' she says. 'I've tried this before and never got the courage to do it. I only dared bring it up to you after I heard you talking to Seth about what happened to you because it made me feel like you'd . . .' – she fidgets with a bracelet she's wearing – 'understand, I guess.'

'A lot of people will understand.' I pause, wondering what else I can do to help her because I want to help her – want to help people who are struggling like I was once. Just thinking about other people out there that have gone through stuff like me and Harper makes me want to find all of them and tell them it'll be okay. I'm not even sure how to do that, but I need to, somehow. 'If you want me to, I can go with you to your appointment.'

'Really?' She perks up, seeming genuinely happy.

I nod. 'Of course.'

She looks utterly relieved. 'Thanks, Callie. And not just for the offer, but for not getting all weirded out. You're really good at this, you know. Talking and understanding and everything.'

Her words warm my heart. 'Thanks. And you're welcome,' I tell her and head for the door. 'Let me know when you get scheduled and if you ever need to talk, I'm right across the room.'

She nods, then I step into the hallway, shut the door behind me, and lean against it. I feel strangely at peace with myself. I'm not even sure if it's because I was able to talk to someone about what happened to me without going into a panic or if it's because I tried to help someone who didn't flat out ask.

'Is everything okay?' Kayden's voice tugs me out of my thoughts.

I turn my head and find him standing to the side of me, the football tucked under his arm. 'Hey, I thought you went down to the car.'

He glances from the door back to me. 'Nah, I thought I'd wait for you here. Seemed like you might need me after whatever was happening in there.'

I stand upright. 'No, I'm fine. She just wanted to talk about stuff.'

'What kind of stuff?' he asks as we move toward the elevator, holding hands.

'Stuff she's going through,' I say vaguely. 'Stuff I'd understand.'

Thankfully, I think he gets what I'm implying without me having to say it aloud, since I'm pretty sure Harper wouldn't want me talking to anyone about it.

I push the down button with my thumb then face him while we wait for the doors to open. 'So are you going to tell me now why you look so happy today?'

'Nope.' His lips twitch with amusement.

'You are the meanest person ever.' I jump into the elevator as the doors swing open, yanking him in with me and he ends up stumbling over his feet. 'But that's okay because I love you.'

He laughs as I stand on my tiptoes to kiss him, but he quickly pulls back when his phone starts buzzing inside the back pocket of his jeans. Usually he ignores calls and texts when we're in a lip lock, so I'm a little surprised when he moves away to take his phone out. He muses over something as he reads the message on the screen.

I recline against the wall and casually ask, 'Who's that?'

He stares at the screen a second longer before texting something back. 'No one.'

I'm not sure how to respond to his brush-off, so I crack a joke. 'Well, clearly it's someone; otherwise, your phone wouldn't have gone off.'

He presses one last button on the screen then returns his phone to his pocket before looking back at me. 'It was just a text from Seth.'

'And what'd it say?'

He shrugs, bracing a hand on the wall beside my head. 'Nothing important really.' He leans in to kiss me, but I place a hand on his solid chest and stop him.

'Your jaw's twitching right now,' I remark, somewhat amused, but a little bit upset.

He gives me a mock offended look, pushing back from the wall to press his hand to his chest. 'Are you accusing me of lying?'

I narrow my eyes at him, but it's a playful gesture. 'Yeah, that's exactly what I'm doing.' I point a finger at him as we reach the bottom floor and the elevator doors glide open. 'I know you're keeping something from me and I'm going to find out.'

He's completely entertained now as he follows me off the elevator and toward the exit doors. 'And how do you plan on doing that?' He shoots me a cocky grin.

'Wow, aren't we a little bit cocky today?' I retaliate with an arrogant squaring of my shoulders as I reach into my pocket. 'But we'll see who's the cocky one after I text Seth.'

His amusement suddenly shifts to worry as I pull out my phone. 'Seth knows he's not supposed to tell you.'

I raise my phone up in front of us and wiggle it around, teasing him. 'Seth is terrible at keeping secrets. You and I both know that.' I really don't have any intention of texting Seth. I'm simply having fun and hoping he'll just tell me whatever his little secret is.

'Callie, don't,' he warns, but he's fighting back a smile.

I let mine slip through, though, full-on grinning as I run backwards toward the door. 'I'm totally doing it.' I laugh, then whirl around and burst through the doors. Snow is tumbling from the sky and the wind is howling, but I continue to sprint down the sidewalk toward the parking lot.

I know he's going to catch me soon, my short legs don't stand a chance against his long, very in-shape ones, but I'm still going to try my hardest because it's fun and I'm enjoying myself. And really that's kind of the point of everything, isn't it? To enjoy life and have fun. I spent so much time never smiling, laughing, enjoying anything, and I feel like I missed out on so much, but that doesn't mean I can't make up for it now, or for the rest of my life, for that matter.

'You think you can outrun me!' Kayden calls out, laughing, his heavy footsteps close behind.

'Of course I can!' Laughter sputters from my lungs

as I veer to the right and try to race across the snowy lawn, but it's chilly enough that the snow is freezing the moment it touches the ground, making it slippery and complicated to run on. I curse as my feet try to part ways from underneath me and my hands shoot out to my sides in an attempt to keep my balance.

Right as I'm about to fall flat on my ass, a set of strong arms wrap around my waist. A split second later, a warm chest presses against my back as I'm helped to my feet.

'You're really asking for it, aren't you?' Kayden whispers in my ear, dragging his teeth across the sensitive spot of flesh right below it as he helps me stand back upright.

I shiver and not from the cold. 'Maybe.'

His fingers dig into my flesh right below the hem of my black T-shirt. 'I'll take your phone as payment for saving your cute little ass from falling.'

I grip my phone in my hand, my eyelashes fluttering against the thick snowflakes. 'No way.'

He chuckles lowly, a deep noise that vibrates from his chest and I have to bite down on my lip to keep from whimpering. 'Okay, I guess we'll have to do this the hard way.'

'Isn't this the hard way already?' I sound breathless.

144

He laughs again and then, without warning, his fingers sneak up my shirt and he starts to tickle me.

'Stop!' I shout through my laughter, my legs giving out on me. I almost buckle to the ground, but he's there to hold me up and he keeps tickling me until I almost pee my pants.

'Fine! I surrender! I surrender!' I gasp through my laughter when I'm about one second away from having an accident.

His fingers instantly stop moving and he kisses the back of my head as he takes the phone from my hand then frees me from his arms.

I spin around and cross my arms over my chest. 'That was cheating.'

He grins proudly as he hides my phone in the pocket of his coat. 'No way. That was completely fair. It's not my fault you're tiny and adorable.' He pokes me in the ribs.

I glare at him, pretending I'm upset. 'If it wasn't for the snow, I would have been able to run faster.'

'Yeah, but I wasn't really running. Just walking swiftly.' He's so smug right now. I've never seen him act like this – so confident. It's sexy and I can't help but jump onto him and kiss him right there in the middle of a blizzard.

He doesn't hesitate, kissing me back with equal hunger, his hands sliding underneath me and cupping my butt. He groans when I bite at his bottom lip, and I gasp as his mouth trails down my jawline, leaving a path of heat simmering against my snow-kissed skin. The mix of heat and ice sends a combustion of sensations swirling through my body. It's blissfully amazing. Mind-blowing. I want more.

'We should go back to your dorm,' I say, my head tipping back as his mouth finds the hollow of my neck. I tangle my fingers through his wet hair and guide him closer. 'Or someplace where we can be alone . . .' I trail off as his phone starts going off in his pocket and this time I'm not as surprised when he breaks the kiss, but am still equally as disappointed.

I sigh, hopping off him as he retrieves his phone. He reads the screen and then grins. 'You know what? That sounds like a great idea,' he says, lacing our fingers together as he tugs me toward the parking lot. 'And I know the perfect place.'

Chapter 14

#155 Welcome Home.

Kayden

It's taken me a couple of weeks to set this up and even longer to get the balls to do it. But after that night I spent with Callie, talking and reliving our past, I knew I had to. I have to give Seth most of the credit, though, for helping me out and for managing to keep it a secret. In the end, it was my speech about how Callie deserved this that won his sworn secrecy.

I'm nervous the entire drive there, not just because I'm not sure how she'll react, but because I'm uncertain how I'll react. It feels like things are moving so quickly suddenly, not just with the relationship between Callie and me, but with life. I feel like sometimes I'm running my hardest to keep up with it, except when I'm with Callie. With

147

Jessica Sorensen

her, I feel like we're walking through it, enjoying every moment together. And that's how I decided.

It was time.

'Where are we?' she asks, leaning forward to get a better look at where we are through the veil of snow hitting the window.

I turn off the car and the wipers stop, making it even harder for her to see. 'It's a surprise.'

'At a park?' she questions as she unfastens her seatbelt.

Nodding, I grab the door handle and push it open. 'Yeah, follow me.'

The park is just part of the surprise. The rest of it is what's right behind the building the park is connected to.

Her perplexity makes this even more entertaining as we get out of the car and she follows me through the snow and around the swing set to the slide. I'm rewarded even more when I start climbing up the ladder and her jaw drops.

'What on earth are you doing?' she asks, dumbfounded, as she watches me climb higher.

I glance over my shoulder back down at her. 'If you want to find out, you're going to have to follow me.'

She eyes the soaking wet ladder with skepticism, but I know she'll do it – she's too brave to let a little wet

148

metal get in her way. And just like I knew she would, she starts up the ladder. When I reach the top, I hop into the tunnel slide and go down it, getting rewarded with a sopping wet puddle at the bottom and a bump on the head from the to-do list I had Seth secure in the slide just before we got here.

Okay, maybe it wasn't the best idea to put it there.

Reaching up, I unhook the string holding it in place and remove the small whiteboard. Seth's erased the entire list, except for number one hundred fifty-five, which might be my favorite number now. I tuck the board into my side, face down so the marker doesn't get smeared by the snow.

'You want me to slide down this?' Callie calls down through the slide with bafflement in her tone.

I lower my head into the slide and yell, 'Hell yes!'

There's a pause and then I hear her squeal as she lowers her feet in then slides down.

'Holy crap!' She jumps up when she reaches the bottom as her ass gets wet. 'That's cold.' Once she gets her footing, she looks from me to what's in my hands. 'What are you holding?'

'Your surprise.' I hand it over, still face down, but it's more because of my nerves than the fear that it'll get wet and ruined.

She rubs her lips together as she raises her brows at me. 'You stole my whiteboard?'

'No. I had Seth borrow it for me.' I tap the back of it, noting that there's a slight tremble to my fingers, something I blame on the snow, completely lying to myself.

A cloud of fog encircles her face as she releases a large exhale. Suddenly, she's nervous, as if she's realized this is no longer a game, but a very serious, life-altering moment.

'I'm afraid to turn it over,' she whispers, but does it anyway.

I hold my breath as I watch her read the two simple, but very momentous words written in red marker, along with the arrow pointing forward at the apartment complex straight across from where we're standing. She must read it a few times because it takes a little bit for her to look up at me.

'Welcome home?' Her brows dip and her head angles to the side as she looks from me to the board, then her gaze tracks the direction of where the arrow is pointing. I know the moment it clicks in her head what I'm trying to say with this whole charade because her breath catches.

'You and Seth are always doing crazy things like this

whenever you ask me out or try to cheer me up,' I tell her and nonchalantly shrug when her gaze locks on mine, even though I'm squirming in my skin. She hasn't shown any signs of being happy and I'm getting worried that maybe this isn't what she really wanted. 'I thought maybe it was my turn' – I brush her hair out of her eyes – 'to do something surprising for you.'

She's silent for what feels like forever, although her eyes never leave mine. It's like she's trying to read my mind or see into my soul or something. If anyone could, it'd be Callie. I just wish I could do the same with her right now, because her quietness is becoming maddening.

'This is what you want?' She gestures at the board then the apartment complex without looking away from me.

I nod. 'More than anything.' Then I hesitate. 'Is this what you want, though?'

She eyes me over for a moment or two longer like she's searching for a hidden answer somewhere inside me. She must find it because suddenly she's dropping the board onto the ground and throwing her arms around me.

'Of course this is what I want.' She hugs me more tightly than one would expect those thin arms of hers to be capable of. 'I've wanted it for a long time.'

I hug her back with everything I have in me. 'I think I have, too, but was afraid to admit it to myself, afraid to let myself have something good.' I pull back to look at her. 'Sorry it took me so long. Do you forgive me?'

'There's nothing to forgive.' She slides her hand down my arm and threads our fingers, beaming as she looks up at me. 'Now, let's go see it.'

I scoop up the now soaked whiteboard and lead the way across the park to the sidewalk where we trot up the stairs of building number three.

When we reach the second floor, I take the key out of my pocket and nervously unlock the door, fumbling a few times before I finally manage it.

'Welcome home,' I say, then push the door open.

Chapter 15

#156 Welcome Home (Yeah, I know it's the same as #155, but it seemed too epic not to get two numbers. Plus, the first time around it got erased).

Callie

'It's really small,' Kayden says as he steps aside to let me enter our apartment. Yes, *our* apartment. 'But it's what we can afford, so . . .' He trails off, ruffling his damp hair into place as he closes the door.

'That's okay.' I take in the space that I'll now call home. It's not furnished yet, so it probably looks bigger than it really is. There's a living room, which I'm standing in, and it's attached to the dining room/kitchen that has a doorway that I assume leads to the bedroom. The space in front of me is about twice the size of the dorms, which sounds big, but it's really not. I don't care, though. At all. 'I could live in a storage room and be okay with it as long as you were there.' I'm starting to sound like one of those sappy romance books, but, oh well – it seems fitting for the moment.

'So you're okay with it?' Kayden stuffs his hands into the pockets of his jeans, appearing anxious. His brown hair still has drops of snow in it and his cheeks are red from the cold, and I just want to throw my arms around him and hug the crap out of him again.

So I do.

'It's perfect,' I tell him, squeezing him tightly so he'll know just how happy I am. His arms circle around me and we share our first hug in our very first home. 'But I have to make sure' – I slant back and tip my chin to look up at him – 'that you're okay with this because we've only been talking about it and then all of a sudden you get a place, and I just want to make sure that it's what you really want because I don't want you to feel pressure or anything. I can wait if I need to.'

He snorts a laugh, and when my brows knit, he says, 'Sorry. It's just that you kind of sounded like a teenage guy right there trying to convince his girlfriend he'll wait to have sex with her.'

My cheeks heat, but I start to think about if he ever

used that line on Daisy and my elation sinks. But then I realize that it doesn't matter what happened with Daisy because he and I are here and he's mine now, not hers.

'You want to show me the bedroom?' I give him my best come-hither look that probably comes off more along the lines of looking confused. At least, that's what I think until his eyes drink me in and he bites at his bottom lip hard.

'You're starting to get a dirty mind.' His smoldering gaze and husky voice sends warm tingles across my skin.

'It must be Seth's influence on me.' My voice is off pitch. 'Sometimes, it's like he's still going through puberty.'

Kayden shakes his head, laughing softly under his breath. 'All right, no more talking. Let's go show you our bedroom.'

We're about halfway across the living room before our lips connect and the clothes start coming off. Shirts are discarded, shoes are kicked off, and we end up leaving a trail of clothing to the bedroom. It's a little chilly in there, but I don't care. Kayden can keep me warm, which is exactly what I tell him as we sink to our knees on the tan carpet and I yank his belt off.

'We should do this every night,' he says, unhooking my bra and pulling it off. 'Only in a bed.'

'No way. We should totally do it on the floor,' I mutter between the kisses he's showering me with on my lips, the arch of my neck, the spot where my heart beats.

He mutters something else, but trails off as my fingers skim down his chest to the top of his jeans. Flicking the button undone, I slip my fingers into his boxers and he groans, biting at my skin.

'Callie . . .' The sound of my name in that raspy voice he uses covers my arms with goose bumps. I become impatient, more than I ever have been before. It's crazy, but the last few weeks have been intense, and I can feel myself changing, becoming more comfortable with myself and who I am with Kayden, so I let my hands wander downward and grasp onto his hardness, something I've never done so boldly before.

'Fuck . . .' He uses that tone again and I seriously can't take it anymore. I'm about to rip his jeans off, literally tear the fabric to bits, when I hear a door open and close from somewhere inside the apartment.

We both freeze, panting for air as we kneel in the center of the room, half naked, our hands grasping at each other.

'Did you hear that?' I whisper, my eyes darting to the door.

Kayden nods, his lips parting, but he's cut off by the sound of a voice.

'Hello, lovebirds,' Seth calls out. 'Are you in here?'

Kayden and mine's eyes widen at the same time. Then suddenly we're scrambling to get our clothes, but it's pointless since we both left our shirts and shoes somewhere between the living room and the hallway. My bra is nearby, though, so I get that on while Kayden does the button of his pants up.

'What should we do?' I whisper. 'My shirt's out there.'

Kayden shrugs, still looking high on the moment. 'Ask him to hand the clothes to us.'

I wrap my arms around myself. 'He'll make a lot of jokes,' I warn.

'He's already going to make jokes,' Kayden states, giving me a sexy half-smile. 'So we might as well go face the music.'

'Knock, knock, knock,' Seth says as he raps his hand on the shut bedroom door. 'Oh, Callie darling, I found something that belongs to you, I think.'

'Oh, leave her alone,' Greyson says. Then the door cracks and he sticks his arm in with our shirts in his hand. 'Here you guys go.'

'Thanks, Greyson.' I take my shirt and hand Kayden his before I put mine on.

Once we're both dressed, we go out together and face the music.

'What are you doing here?' I ask as we walk into the living room.

Greyson's looking around at our kitchen and Seth is observing the small patio attached to the living room through a sliding glass door.

'I came to see how things went,' Seth says, turning to face us. 'And to see if you guys wanted to go have dinner and celebrate.' He takes in the sight of us; messy hair, wrinkled shirts, and my zippers undone. 'But I'm guessing it went well, considering how hot and bothered you two look right now, thanks to my interruption.' He flashes me an unapologetic grin.

'We can go,' Greyson tells me, taking Seth's hand and pulling him toward the door. Greyson's always been the more level-headed of the two and tries to keep Seth intact when he can. 'In fact, we should go and give you two some privacy.'

'No, it's okay. We were finished anyway.' I don't mean for it to come out how it sounded and I feel a little embarrassed.

'You were?' Kayden cocks an eyebrow. 'Because I wasn't.'

My embarrassment doubles and I playfully swat his arm, hoping it'll divert everyone's attention from my blushing.

'It's okay. We can go get dinner,' Kayden says through his chuckles then his gaze fastens on mine. '*We* can finish later.'

All three of them laugh and I should get even more embarrassed, but I find myself calmer than anything. Because this is what life is about, I think. Moments like these.

Right now, everything is perfect.

Chapter 16

#103 Keep Trying to Outrun Your Demons.

Kayden

The next day I have a game. I'm excited and nervous and afraid, but that's how it always is for me. There's always a list of things I could mess up on flowing through my head and a list of things I can do not to fuck up. But sometimes I just wish I could get the lists to stop and just play, because I love the game.

I play pretty fucking well through almost the entire game, but only when it veers toward the end does it really matter. The crowd is going wild. Everyone is screaming, hollering, cheering me on, including Callie, Seth, and Greyson, who I know are sitting close to the front, supporting me like they always do. There are players lined up on both sides, me at the back, ready to catch the snap. The lights are bright above me, but there's a shadow cast over me that no one else can see. We're one touchdown away from winning and there's less than a minute on the clock. The pressure is on me to do well; my teammates, my coach, the entire stadium waiting for me to make the perfect throw. But it's small in comparison to the voice I hear in my head.

My father's.

It's gotten worse since Dylan found him, now shouting instead of whispering.

Run!

Make the perfect throw!

Win the fucking game!

I hear the snap.

Feel the rush.

Here the scream.

You better make this!

It echoes through my head.

I feel the ball touch my hands and I run back, searching for an opening. My heart is pounding in my chest as players move around the field and I'm aware of them all. But not as aware as I am of the voice inside my head.

You better not fuck this up!

There's no clean throw.

Everyone is covered.

The clock is ticking.

My heart is pounding.

You better not mess this up, Kayden!

I move to the right, and run, my feet hammering against the grass as I focus on one thing – outrunning that damn voice. My feet move faster than they ever have as I dodge to the left then the right. There are people in front of me, behind me, coming at me from different directions, but I focus on the end zone. It's all that matters. And as the clock continues to tick, a player grabbing at me from the back, I jump across that line.

Touchdown!

The crowd goes crazy! My team goes crazy! Everyone is running at me. We won! We won! We won!

But I feel like I've lost somehow because in the end I can still hear that damn voice.

You could have done better.

After I'm showered and changed, I head out of the locker room even though my team's begging me to go out.

'Come on, man,' Tyrel Buliforton, the end back,

says as I sling my bag over my shoulder and head for the door. 'You played fucking awesome. We need to go celebrate.'

I shake my head. 'Nah, I already got plans,' I lie because all I want to do is find Callie and hold her, knowing it'll help me leave the voice of my father behind.

'For someone who made the winning touchdown, you sure look super depressed,' Luke Price, my best friend, says as he follows me out of the locker room, zipping up his coat. Luke's been my best friend since we were kids and has his own problems with his parents. We don't talk about it, though. I think he saves it for his girlfriend, Violet, just like I do with Callie.

'You're not going out either,' I tell him as we step outside and into the cold.

He shrugs. 'Partying isn't . . . or can't be my thing anymore, being a recovering alcoholic and all.'

'You doing okay with that?' I ask, tugging my fingers through my damp hair as I search for Callie in the crowd of people loitering around, wearing the school colors.

'Yeah, but I know myself enough to know that I'll be doing okay just as long as I go home and not out.' He stuffs his hands into his pockets and then grins as he spots Violet leaning against a post not too far from us. It's funny, but he never really smiles except for when he's with her.

I wonder if it's the same way with me when I'm with Callie.

As if to answer my own question, Callie emerges from the crowd, shoving her way through the last of the people, and a big smile rises on my face.

'Hey you,' she says, rushing up to me as some guy hoots and hollers from the crowd. 'You played great.'

'Yeah . . . I could have done a little better, though.' I wrap my arms around her when she reaches me and I pull her tight against me. Her warmth spreads across my body and I breathe in the peace.

'You did perfect,' she whispers in my ear and then leans back. 'We should celebrate.'

'I did okay,' I press. 'Not perfect.'

Her lips curve to a frown. 'No sulking or I'll have to force you to do fun things until you're laughing so hard you pee your pants.'

I laugh at her, brushing the pad of my thumb across her bottom lip. 'All right, you win,' I say. 'I played perfect.'

Her lips turn upward again and there's a sparkle in her eyes that matches the stars above us. 'You fucking kicked ass.'

I can't help myself. I bust up laughing. Callie rarely swears, so when she does, it's hilarious. 'Oh my God, it's so funny when you say fuck.'

She grins, but her cheeks turn the slightest shade of pink. 'I knew that one would get you to laugh.'

'You always manage to,' I say, no longer finding our conversation funny but personal and intimate. 'And actually I was thinking we could pick up takeout and then go hang out at our place.'

'Our place.' She says the words slowly, letting them roll off her tongue. 'That sounds like a great idea to me to celebrate if that's okay. Maybe Luke and Violet could come hang.'

I glance over at the two of them chatting near the front of the crowd. 'It might be nice now that you and Violet are getting along.'

Callie nods. 'Sounds perfect.' She threads her fingers through mine and pulls me away from the stadium – away from my father's voice – and by the time we reach the car, it's disappeared completely.

I just wish it would stay that way.

Chapter 17

#157 Get to Know Your Family Even When It Seems Impossible.

Kayden

Callie and I managed to move in a few things before we had to part ways for Thanksgiving, but between work and school, we still have a ways to go. We do get to spend one night in our apartment together, cuddled up on a blanket and watching movies on my laptop, before she drops me off at the airport so I can fly out to Virginia for Thanksgiving.

I'm not happy about spending the holiday without her, but I understand she needs to go home and see her brother while I need to go see mine. It's part of growing and getting better, I guess — learning how to do things on your own. I just wish doing things on my own meant I could still hold Callie's hand because it feels weird without her near me.

Dylan's wife – who insists I call her Liz, instead of by her full name, which is Elizabeth – is freaking out, trying to get the house in order for her parents' arrival, while she tries to cook everything all at once. The kitchen smells like burnt toast and the air is heavy with smoke, causing the smoke detectors to go off sporadically.

'Does she need help?' I ask Dylan. We're sitting at the table playing cards, which blows my freaking mind because it's so normal and makes me uncomfortable, since I'm not used to it. What I'm used to – at least, the last time I was at a family event – is yelling, fighting, hitting, breaking.

Dylan assesses his cards as he takes a gulp of his beer. 'You can ask her, but she'll flip out on you.' He sets two cards face down on the table and gives himself two more from the deck. Dylan looks a lot like me; brown hair, tall, with a medium build, and is probably my future. Well, except the whole teaching thing. I can't see myself doing that. Honestly, I'm not sure I can picture myself doing this either, sitting at the table while Callie cooks dinner. It seems so fucking rude to make her do it. Plus, Callie doesn't like to cook very much.

'Do you need any help?' I finally ask as Liz rushes back and forth between the stove and a bowl she's mixing something in. She's got blonde hair, blue eyes, and is wearing an apron over her jeans and T-shirt, and she doesn't look very comfortable in the kitchen.

She waves me off, scurrying for a towel when she spills milk on the counter. 'No. You're the guest and you should sit back and relax.'

Dylan chuckles under his breath as he rearranges the cards in his hand. 'Don't worry. She's going to give up here in about a half an hour and we'll end up going out.'

'So, this is your tradition?' I examine my cards. I don't have a very good hand, but we're not playing for money, just fun. I know why, too. When we were younger, our father would make us play for money. If he won, he'd take all his winnings and if he lost, he'd beat the shit out of us because in his words, 'we were cheating bastards'. So really, we'd always lose.

Dylan nods, laying his cards down and I do the same. I think I like Dylan a little bit more when instead of bragging about winning, he says, 'Yeah, if she'd just let me help, though, it wouldn't be a problem. I'm an excellent cook.'

As Liz whisks by the table, she whips Dylan in the side with the dish towel she's carrying. 'That's such a lie. You equally suck at cooking, which is why we have at least five takeout places on speed dial.'

'One for each weekday?' I joke, gathering the cards. Liz nods with a serious look on her face and it kind of makes me smile because they have their own thing going here that doesn't seem at all like my parents. They're not nasty to each other. They smile. Laugh.

It's nice, and kind of a relief because it gives me the tiniest ray of hope that I won't turn out like my father, that I can have this normalcy, this happiness, that I can have a future filled with what I want, and with who I want.

'You want to go watch the game?' Dylan asks, nodding at the living room as he picks up his beer and scoots his chair back from the table.

'Sure.' I get up and we wander into the living room and settle on the leather couch in front of the flat screen. The wall is covered with photos of the two of them – at their wedding, the beach, on the top of a mountain. It makes me sad because I don't have any photos where I look happy. Callie and I don't even have any photos of us on the wall.

'So, you think you're ever going to do this?' Dylan asks after we sit in silence through a couple of plays.

'Do what?' I ask, tipping my head back to take a sip of my soda.

He picks at the damp label on the beer bottle. 'Play professionally . . .' He leans forward to set the beer on the coffee table, then turns to face me, leaning against the arm rest. 'Liz says you're pretty good.'

I drum my fingers against the side of the soda can, a pucker forming at my brow. 'When has she seen me play?'

'She watches your games on the internet.'

'All of them?' I'm dumbfounded. She watches me play? Really? Why?

'Most of them,' he says. 'And I've watched a few, too. I'd watch more, but I'm working on getting my master's degree right now, so I don't have a lot of free time.' He gives me a pat on the arm. 'Don't look so surprised. We care about you, Kayden.' Suddenly, the mood shifts as he blows out a loud breath. 'I know it might seem like I don't, since we didn't talk for years, but if I had known what was going on in that house . . . that he'd gotten *that* bad . . . that he would actually try . . .' He can't even get the words out and he ends by giving up, raking his fingers through his hair before he says, 'I wouldn't have been absent for so long. I shouldn't have and it's one of my biggest regrets.'

'I kind of understand why you did it, though,' I say, staring at the soda in my hand. 'I had a hard time just coming here . . . The whole family thing is strange to me because it's good, yet it reminds me of how bad things can be. And I don't mean you. You were never bad. And Tyler, well, he was great until he started doing drugs and turned into a mess. But I mean Mom and Dad.'

Dylan reaches for his beer again. 'It is hard, isn't it? It took me forever to figure out how to be in a house with Liz, how to act like a family because I didn't have a freaking clue. I felt so lost, you know?'

'And now?' I wonder. 'Is it better now . . .? Because it seems like it is.'

He nods. 'Now I'm happy.' He gives me a smile then takes a sip of the beer before he asks, 'So what about you, Kayden? Are you happy?'

I shrug. 'Sure. I guess.'

He frowns. 'You guess?'

I shrug again. 'Sometimes I am, but I wish I could figure out how to be all the time, you know.' He gives me a sad look and I explain further. 'It's just that I have no idea what I want to do with my life. I mean, football's great and I'm good at it and enjoy playing it, but I only got into it because of Dad. And that's the thing. It all . . .' I blow out a breath. 'It all comes back to him. I don't want to have anything to do with him and every time something is connected to him, I'm not happy . . . I swear to God, I can sometimes hear his voice in my head when I'm out playing . . . I just want to be able to play for me . . .' I stop talking, unsure why I decided to say that aloud – I haven't even told Callie about that yet.

Dylan's shoulders slump, probably from the weight of the memories of our father. 'Kayden, you shouldn't let that – *him* – stop you from doing anything. It only gives him more power over your life. If football makes you happy, then do it. I know it's hard, but you need to let this thing with Dad go. Let the past go. And I think once you do, you'll stop hearing all that fucked-up shit he said to you all the time – you'll be able to play for you.'

'You pretty much just stated word for word what my therapist said,' I tell him, then heave a heavy sigh. 'And I know I should . . . and I'm trying to. It's just going to take some time for me to figure shit out.' I set the can down on the table, then cross my arms as I recline on the sofa, wondering if there will ever be a time I can play for me and just love/love the game. I sure as hell hope so. 'I have a ways to go, though . . . I mean, I still fuck up sometimes with certain things.' I'm not going to go any further than that, as I'm not ready to talk to him about my cutting disorder.

'Everyone does that. It's called life, Kayden.'

'Yeah, I know.'

A gap of silence goes by and I start to focus back on the game. Someone just scored a touchdown and the crowd is going wild. The sight puts me in a state of contentment, like it does whenever I'm playing.

'What about that Callie girl you're dating?' he asks, drawing my attention back to him. 'Are you still seeing her?'

I move to grab my soda. 'Yeah, we actually just got our own place right before I headed out here.'

His eyes widen in astonishment. 'Shut the fuck up. Seriously?' he asks and I nod, caught off guard by his excitement. 'Wow, I didn't know you guys were that serious. You never really seemed like you were on the phone. Then again, you barely talk about your private life either, so . . .' He trails off, looking sort of sad.

'Don't take that personally,' I say. 'I only talk about that stuff with Callie.'

He nods, relaxing a little. 'Wow, you are fucking serious with this girl, aren't you?'

'Who's serious with a girl?' Liz interrupts our conversation as she comes strolling in with a plate full of what looks like burnt squash. I didn't even know you could burn squash.

'Kayden,' Dylan tells her at the same time I say, 'No one.'

Dylan's grin is conniving as he looks from me to Liz. 'Callie and Kayden moved in together.'

'Really?' Her eyes light up as she sets the plate down on the coffee table. 'That's so huge, Kayden. Why didn't you tell us?'

Again, Dylan looks hurt and it makes me feel slightly remorseful. Maybe I've been going about this whole getting-to-know-your-family thing all wrong. Maybe I shouldn't have been shutting them out as much as I have been. But it's difficult to let people in when I know how bad people can hurt you. Still, I decide to try because I know if Callie were here, that's what she'd want me to do.

'Sorry, I think it just slipped my mind. I'm not used to telling people things, I guess.'

'Well, that I do get,' he says, nervously cracking his knuckles. 'I've actually been needing to talk to you about something.'

I can tell by his tone what it's about. 'You found out more about our parents, didn't you?'

'I got a call from Mom this morning, but I've been procrastinating about telling you because I didn't want to ruin the trip. But I guess we're never going to have much of a relationship if we don't start talking to each other, are we?' he asks, and even though I'm not too thrilled to hear more about Mom and Dad, I nod. He wavers, uncertainty filling his expression. 'She actually wanted to tell me about our father.' Another long pause as he squirms in the chair. 'It's bad, Kayden. Dad, I mean . . . he's in bad shape.'

I'm fairly sure an entire set of commercials plays before I'm able to get ahold of my voice and my emotions enough to respond. 'How bad?'

Resolution.

This is what you wanted, right?

You are a terrible person.

'Really, really bad,' Dylan says, releasing an exhausted breath.

It's strange, but it seems like we should be crying or something, yet our eyes are dry. My heart feels the same way, too, and those thoughts of how I've got to be a bad person come rushing back to me because this can't be normal – to feel nothing toward the person who raised you. Regardless, that's how I feel.

Absolutely nothing.

'I think he's going to die,' Dylan says quietly.

And again, nothing.

I think Callie might have been wrong because there's no way I'm not broken.

Chapter 18

#159 Don't Panic When Things Get Brutally Ugly.

Callie

It's the day after Thanksgiving and the house I grew up in is already sparkling with Christmas lights, a tree in need of decorating, and tons of cut-out snowflakes. My mother is one of those people who *loves* the holidays to the point where it might be an unhealthy obsession. However, after years and years of it, my brother, father, and I have learned to tolerate it. We've also learned how to avoid countless hours of trimming the tree with silver balls and tinsel.

'I can't believe she bought your lie this time,' my brother Jackson says from the front seat of my father's truck as he fidgets with the stereo. 'Telling her we're going to buy some replacement bulbs for the lights, even though all of them are up. I still can't believe you actually took a couple of the bulbs out so some wouldn't work.'

Jackson looks better than he used to; less stoner/pothead and more hipster. He's been attending community college in Florida where my grandparents live and works as a manager at an electronic store. I'm glad to see him like this, instead of the druggie jerk he was when he had spent so much time with Caleb.

My father chuckles as he turns the wipers up a notch. 'I've been having to get more creative with my excuses to get out of the house. Picking up Callie was a long one.' He grins at me from over his shoulder. 'And a good one, too.'

I smile back then watch the snowflakes splatter against the window. The snow hasn't let up since he picked me up from Laramie three days ago. No one I knew was going that way and Kayden was worried his car wasn't safe enough to get me there with how bad the roads have been. When I told my dad this, he not only got excited to come get me, but he also remarked what a great guy Kayden was for thinking of my safety.

'You've been awfully quiet,' my father says as he makes a right down Main Street.

'That's because she's lovesick.' Jackson smirks at me and I stick out my tongue.

'Is that what it is?' my father asks and I vow to get Jackson back for bringing this up. 'Do you miss Kayden?'

'Of course I miss him,' I say, unzipping my coat because Jackson is overheating the car with how high he's got the heater turned up. 'But I'm always this quiet.'

'That's true,' Jackson mumbles. He folds his arms and stares out the window at the buildings bordering the street. The town is small, but it's the day after Thanksgiving and the sales the stores are having are causing havoc in the streets.

'We should go snowboarding or something this weekend,' Jackson suddenly says to me. I know what he's doing. Ever since I told my family about what happened with Caleb on my twelfth birthday, Jackson has acted almost too nice. I think he feels guilty because Caleb was his friend and therefore was in the house because of him. I don't blame him, though. It's not like he knew it was going to happen. Caleb had everyone fooled.

'I don't really know how to snowboard,' I admit as our dad turns into the busy parking lot of the hardware store located in the heart of the town. 'And I don't have a board.'

'You can borrow my old one. And we'll go down the small hill.'

I frown. 'You mean the bunny hill?'

He unclicks his seatbelt. 'See, you already know the lingo. You'll be fine.'

I roll my eyes but agree to go. Then the three of us hop out of the car and face the madness of the store. There's so many people there that we have to stand in a line just to get in.

'Wow, people are crazy,' Jackson mumbles, tugging the hood of his coat over his head as we wait to get to the doors. 'You should have thought of something else, Dad, that didn't require going into stores.'

'Yeah, you're probably right,' he agrees, putting on a pair of gloves. 'But I panicked when she came at me with the inflatable Santa.'

I'm laughing at him when my phone vibrates from inside my pocket. I take it out as we move forward with the line, already guessing who the text is from.

And I'm right.

Kayden: So how's it going?

Me: Super great, except for the whole avoid-crazy-

mom thing turned into an enter-crazy-shopper thing.

Kayden: ???

Me: My dad makes up an excuse every year to get us out of the house while my mother goes mad ninja Christmas crazy on the house. But this time he didn't put enough thought into it because he took us to the store. And people are nuts. There's a line just to get into the store.

Kayden: I'm sorry you're not having fun :(

Me: I actually am. It's good to see my dad and Jackson. He actually offered to take me snow-boarding this weekend.

Kayden: U should go. It's a lot of fun.

Me: I told him I would, but I'm pretty sure I'll just spend the day falling on my butt.

Kayden: At least you'll look adorable doing it ;)

Me: Hmm . . . I'm not so sure. I think my ador-ableness is only seen by your eyes.

Kayden: No way. U just don't see it.

I'm about to text back when I realize Jackson and my dad are staring at me with silly grins on their faces.

'What?' I ask them.

Jackson sniggers, shaking his head, while my dad just continues to smile. 'It's nothing.' He turns forward and moves with the line. We're almost there. 'How's Kayden doing?'

'Good. But how'd you know I was texting him?' I wonder, pulling my hood over my head as the wind picks up.

'Because you have that lovesick, puppy-dog look in your eyes,' Jackson says smugly as we finally, FINALLY make it into the store.

'I do not,' I protest as another text comes through my phone. I have to keep my elbows tucked in while I type just to avoid getting slammed into.

Kayden: U still there.

Me: Yeah, my dad and Jackson interrupted. Sorry.

Kayden: So other than shopping, how's your day going?

My dad takes one look at the congested aisles and then gives a loud clap of his hands. 'All right, who's ready for this?' When neither Jackson nor I respond, he claps his hands again then leans down like we're in a huddle. 'All right, Jackson. You go up the left aisle and to the back to get the bulbs. Callie, I'm out of staples, too, so you go right, go about halfway to the back of the store then make another right. I'll go get in line and save us a spot so we're not waiting all day.' He claps his hands for a third time then says, 'Break.'

Jackson and I trade an oh-my-God look because we're so used to this. Growing up with a father who's a high-school football coach, everything's about the game. Still, we head off to our designated areas, splitting apart and shoving our way through the crazed shoppers. As I make my way to the aisle, I text Kayden back.

Me: Good. Nothing too exciting is going on. Well, except for the fact that my dad just made Jackson and I huddle up so he could give as a play by play of how we were going to get through the store.

Kayden: Must be the coach in him.

Me: I guess so. Or that he's just getting crazier with old age.

Kayden: God, I wish I could be there. I miss u so fucking bad.

Me: I miss you, too. Is everything ok?

Kayden: Yeah. Actually things are good. Liz ended up burning the dinner, but we ate at this really nice place. And Dylan and I have been talking a lot. I even got to see Tyler for a day and he seemed a lot better.

Me: What about your parents? Have u heard anything more?

It takes him a little while to answer. And by the

183

time the text comes through, I've made it to the shelf with a small selection of staples on it.

Kayden: Yeah. Dylan talked to my mom a little bit yesterday. My dad's in really bad shape. Not sure if he's going to make it. My mother's still not saying how he got there in the first place. But I found out they're in North Carolina.

I'm shocked. Not going to make it? Oh my God, how do I even respond to that? Normally, I'd feel really sorry, but I know from the conversation I had with Kayden in the car, his feelings about all this are buried in confusion created by years of physical abuse.

Me: I'm so sorry. Do u want me to call u when I get out of the store?

I grab a box of staples and turn to leave the aisle, ready to get out of there so I can hear well enough to call Kayden and make sure he's doing okay. I'm distracted by my phone, not paying attention to where I'm going, and I end up slamming into someone.

The box of staples and my phone slip from my fingers. 'Shit,' I curse, bending down to pick them up. 'Sorry about that.'

'Don't worry about it.'

The sound of the voice sends the hairs on the back of my neck on end. I haven't heard that voice in over a year. It's a voice I wish I'd never heard to begin with, wish to God I wasn't hearing now.

'Fuck,' I mutter under my breath, scrambling to pick up my phone and the staples without looking at Caleb. *He can't be here. He can't be here.*

He just can't.

But he is, something I painfully have to acknowledge after I collect my stuff and stand back up. He's right in front of me, wearing that stupid look on his face, the one that says he thinks he has control over me.

But he doesn't anymore.

I do.

'What the fuck are you doing here?' I'm surprised at how steady my voice is. I make myself carry his gaze, but those dark eyes of his are still hard to look at it.

'Wow, you've developed quite the mouth on you,' he says. He looks rundown, bags under his eyes, holes in his jeans and the oversized coat he's wearing nearly swallows his thin body. This isn't the Caleb I used to know, but he still sends my heart racing with fear. 'That's two fucks and a shit that's left your lips in the last minute. The Callie I used to know couldn't even say crap without getting flustered.'

'The Callie you knew doesn't exist anymore.' I suck

in a breath, feeling my heart trembling in my chest. 'And honestly, you never really knew her.'

'Didn't I?' His gaze flicks across my body. I'm not wearing anything revealing – jeans, a coat, and boots – but suddenly I feel like I'm standing in front of him with my Halloween costume on, vulnerable as if he's seeing all of me. And it's not for him to see. Ever again!

'I'm leaving.' I dodge to the side to swing around him. I'll go find my dad and Jackson where I know I'll be safe, and then call the cops. Caleb violated his probation when he skipped town after drug charges were pressed against him, so he's in trouble. I just wish it was for what he did to me.

Before I can skitter around him, he shuffles to the side and blocks my path. There are a couple of people nearby, but they're too distracted by bright neon sale stickers to notice what's going on. Or they're just too afraid to do anything about it.

'Relax, Callie. I just want to talk.' His lips curl to a smirk, revealing the monster side of him. This is what he's always done to me, tried to torture me and get under my skin just by looking at me. I think he actually enjoys seeing me panic, but I'm not going to give him the satisfaction of it like I used to.

Standing up straight, I turn to head in the opposite direction. However, things get brutally ugly as he snatches hold of my arm and his fingers dig through the fabric of my coat. A fire and a chill whirl through me simultaneously, the chill stemming from my fear, but the fire giving me anger, giving me strength.

Without even flinching, I whirl around and shove him back with the pent-up rage of the last seven years. 'Don't fucking touch me.' My voice is calm but firm as he stumbles back in shock. I don't wait for him to say anything because I don't care what he has to say.

Nothing that he does matters.

He's not part of my life anymore.

I'm in control.

I am strong.

Still, by the time I make it to where my dad and Jackson are, I'm on the verge of crying. Not because I'm afraid, but because I'm so angry.

'Shit, Callie. What's wrong?' Jackson asks as I rush up to them.

'Call the police. Tell them Caleb's here,' I say, wiping my tears away with the back of my hand. People are staring at me like I'm crazy, but right now, I don't care. I just care about getting out of this store.

'Did he hurt you?' Jackson asks, then takes off in

187

the direction I just came from without waiting for my response. 'I'm going to beat his ass.'

I snag the sleeve of his coat before he can get too far. 'He didn't hurt me. Just call the police, okay? It's way better than beating his ass and then you getting in trouble for it.'

He glances back and forth between the aisles and me, conflicted. Eventually, he gives in. 'Fine.' He takes out his phone, muttering, 'Dumb fuck must be hiding out at his parents' house.' He storms off toward the doors, shoving people out of his way as he puts the phone to his ear.

I try to breathe quietly, but I start to struggle for air. I keep scanning the store for signs of Caleb, waiting for him to appear again.

Finally, my dad removes the staples from my trembling hand and sets them and the bulbs down on the nearest rack. 'We can wait to get those,' he says, then puts an arm around me and steers me out the doors to the truck, even though I can tell that, like Jackson, he wants to turn around and beat the crap out of Caleb.

He asks me a thousand times if I'm okay. Jackson does the same thing when he gets off the phone. I keep telling them yes because I really am okay. Yeah,

Caleb is a horrible person who did horrible things, but I stood up for myself finally. I didn't panic, didn't let him win.

It's taken me seven years to get to this place, and even though I'm still terrified, I'm also strong. Stronger than I used to be.

Stronger than the monster.

Chapter 19

#160 Get To Her – Get Home No Matter What.

Kayden

It's the day after Thanksgiving and I'm sitting on the sofa, watching some television with Dylan and Liz, and texting Callie on and off during the commercials. It's been both a rough but decent day as we all struggle through our feelings about my dad being in a coma while trying to enjoy each other's company. I don't think any of us knows what to do with the information about my father, so we've all just sort of been quiet, afraid to be the first one to speak, to say what we're all thinking – that we might not be as upset as we should be. I could see it in Dylan's eyes the more we talked and in Tyler's eyes, too, which were less hazy than the last time I saw them. We didn't get to visit him for too long, but it was nice to see him when he was not high and out of his mind. He kind of reminded me of the Tyler I knew who taught me how to ride a bike, not the one that took off and left to become a drug addict.

'I'm going to go make some popcorn,' Liz announces during a commercial, getting up from the couch. 'Kayden, do you need anything?'

I shake my head. 'No, I'm good.' I take out my phone and text Callie again. She hasn't responded to my last two texts and I'm starting to wonder what's up. It's making me uneasy, but that feeling could also be stemming from the fact I'm under a lot of emotional stress and haven't picked up a razor yet.

Me: Hey, it's me again. R u okay? I'm starting to get worried.

I hold my phone for a while, waiting for a text to come through, but instead it starts to ring. Callie's name flashes across the screen and a smile touches my lips as I get up and go back to the guestroom where I've been spending my nights.

'I'm glad you called,' I say, shutting the door behind me. I don't bother turning the lamp on, since the sun's still up enough to light up the room. 'I was starting to get a little worried.'

'I know you were,' she replies remorsefully. 'Sorry. I should have called sooner.' There's an edge to her voice and I know right away that something's not right.

'Something is wrong' – I shove some of my dirty clothes out of the way then lie down on the bed – 'isn't there?'

She lets out a shaky breath. 'Kind of. I mean, everything's okay now.'

My body goes rigid. 'But it wasn't a while ago?'

'No, not really.'

I hesitate, unsure if I should ask because of the reluctant tone she has. 'Do you . . .? Do you want to talk about it?'

'Not really,' she sighs. 'But I probably should.' Another sigh. Then another. It's driving me mad knowing something happened, but not knowing what. 'I ran into Caleb today.' Her voice is barely a whisper.

I bolt upright from the bed, completely taken off guard. 'What? Where?' My hands ball into fists and I have to stab my nails into my palms to keep myself from losing it. I need to calm down. Need to de-stress somehow because I'm feeling that pull again, toward my razor . . . my flesh . . . the pain . . . the blood . . . the relief. I squeeze my eyes shut. 'Please, tell me you're okay.'

'I'm fine, Kayden. I promise. I just ran into him at the store while I was texting you. It's why I stopped.' Her pause seems to last forever. 'I'm okay, though. I totally stood up to him and even shoved him when he tried to grab me.'

'He tried to grab you?' I'm so angry I have to pry my nails away from my palms and grab onto a nearby throw pillow to grip the shit out of it. 'In a fucking store?'

'Yes, but it's okay,' Callie says quickly. 'I got to stand up to him like I've always wanted to do. And Jackson called the cops and they arrested him. God, I can't believe he's behind bars.' She sounds happy about it, but I'm not, still stuck on the part where he put his freaking hands on her.

'I want to beat the shit out of him right now,' I admit, chucking the pillow at the wall, 'for touching you.'

'But you don't need to this time,' she says proudly. 'I took care of him myself. I stood up to him and Jackson called the police and he was arrested for the drug charges pressed against him last year, so he might end up in jail. And I know it's in no way enough for what he did to me, but it still feels like I'm getting a little bit of resolution.'

'Callie . . .' I struggle with what to say, with what to do, with how to calm myself down, and not have another slip up.

'Kayden . . .' Her tone is way lighter than one would expect it to be. How can she be so calm? While I'm a wreck? And it doesn't even have anything to do with me.

'Tell me what to do,' I say in a strained whisper. 'I need to do something, otherwise I'm going to lose it.'

'You can tell me about how you are,' she suggests. 'I need the distraction.'

'Really? That's all you need.'

'Yes.'

'I can do that.' I blow out a breath and try to relax and tell her about my trip, even though I've already texted her about the majority of it. But she asked me to do it and that's all that really matters at the moment. Not *my* need to beat Caleb or *my* rage. It's not a *my* thing, but about *her*.

After I've yammered her ear off for about an hour, long enough that the sun is slowly descending behind the mountains, I stop to give her some time to speak, asking her what her plans are, besides snowboarding with her brother.

'Well, I should probably tell you I'm heading back

to Laramie tomorrow morning,' she says and I can hear her typing on her computer, probably writing either a story for class or an article for her internship.

'But I thought you weren't going back until Monday morning?' I slip my shoes off and kick them off the bed.

'Yeah, but Jackson wants me to show him all the fun partying stuff to do in Laramie on Saturday and then hit some slopes down there on Sunday. Honestly, I'm ready to get out of this town. As much fun as I've had decking out the Christmas tree, I miss our home.'

I smile as I lean against the headboard and stretch out my legs. 'I miss our home, too, but I have to ask, *you* showing *Jackson* the party scene? Really?'

She laughs and it's the most serene sound I've ever heard, like what music does to some people. 'Yeah, crazy, right? I'd worry I'd disappoint, but he seems to have chilled out on the partying and I think it's been a while, so I'm hoping that means it won't take a lot for him to have fun. Plus, Luke and Violet are there.'

I can't contain my laughter. 'So you, Luke, Violet, and Jackson are all going to hang out?'

'Hey, I'm friends with them, too,' she protests, offended. 'And I already texted Luke to tell him what's up and he said he was down to chill.'

'I know you're friends with them.' I let my laughter die down. 'Sorry, it was just a little unexpected. I'm sure you'll have fun, although I'm jealous I can't be there.'

'I'm sorry you can't either, but I'm totally going to have fun,' she says mischievously. 'I'm going to wear that dress I wore on Halloween and be a party animal.'

'No way. No wearing that dress without me around.'

'You sound jealous.'

'I am.'

'You should come home early, too, then, and I'll put on the dress for you.' She pauses. 'Or maybe I'll just wear the boots and nothing else.'

I bite down on my lip hard, a growl rising in my throat. 'Are you trying to entice me with your sexiness?'

'Maybe.' The naughtiness in her voice is making me go rock hard. 'Is it working?'

I have to adjust myself as I picture her in what she's describing. 'Fuck yeah. I'm hard as hell.'

I hear her catch her breath from the other end and can picture her blushing. 'So do you think you can swing it?'

'Doing you in those boots?' I ask. 'Hell yeah.'

She snorts a laugh. 'No. I mean come home early.'

God, what I would give to be home with her, especially after what happened with Caleb. Regardless if she says she's okay, I still need to see for myself – be there for her. But how?

'I wish I could, but I'm not sure I could afford to switch flights.' I sigh. It's not like I want to get away from my brother, I just miss her. Things are starting to get to me here, and I know if I was with her, it wouldn't be as hard to deal with.

'Yeah, I know. You probably shouldn't either.' She sighs. 'I was just being selfish.'

'You weren't being selfish. You're allowed to want me.'

Her soft laughter vibrates through my ear and makes me want to be near her even more. 'Well, I want you all the time, but I guess if I have to, I can wait until Monday.' She pauses and I hear someone saying something. 'Sorry, but I have to go. Mom wants me to come help her bake pies.' She sounds less than thrilled about it.

'Have fun,' I tease because I know she hates baking.

'Ha, ha.' She doesn't find me funny at all. 'I love you.'

My heart swells inside my chest. Those words will never get old and I want to hear them in person where

I can kiss her right after they're uttered. 'I love you, too.'

The silence gets to me the moment I hang up, as my problems, along with what happened with Callie, come rushing back to me. I feel so alone, so confused, so in need of seeing her, just to make sure she's okay. I'm tempted to do things to get my mind off the emotional overload. There are only two things I feel like doing right now – seeing Callie and picking up my razor. And one seems so much easier to do at the moment than the other.

Chapter 20

#161 Go Home When You Need To. There's No Shame in Leaving Early.

Kayden

I wasn't planning on leaving early, even though I really fucking want to. I'd told myself to stick this out, that Callie would be okay, but for some reason, I couldn't shake the feeling that things were about to change.

That something bad was about to happen.

Call it years of getting these feelings right before my father would get set off. I guess he somehow built an alarm inside me.

For the most part, the day is going good. We're sitting around, playing Scrabble, laughing about the perverted word my brother just laid down and got forty-something points for – cock.

'God, I feel like I'm married to a teenage boy,' Liz says, throwing a chip at Dylan, who laughs when it pegs him in the forehead.

'You like my dirty mind,' he replies. 'Don't lie.'

She's about to snap a comeback when the phone rings. And we all just sort of freeze.

I'm not even sure why we do. It's not like we know who's calling, or maybe we do. Maybe there is some sort of silent forewarning we all picked up on, like the silent alarm inside me.

I can tell Dylan doesn't want to answer it, but he does. And within thirty seconds, his skin pales. Whatever it is, it is bad.

He seems lost for words, tugging his fingers through his hair as he nods and slumps back in his chair. 'Uh. Okay.'

I'm watching him like a hawk, waiting for him to show a sign that will let me know what the fuck is going on.

'Kayden, why don't you come help me move the sofa,' Liz suddenly says, pushing back from the table. 'I've been dying to rearrange the living room and could use an extra pair of strong arms.'

I don't bother pointing out that it'd be easier if Dylan and I moved it, since clearly she's trying to get me out of the kitchen and away from Dylan and the phone call.

'Okay . . .' I hesitantly get up from the chair and follow her out of the kitchen and into the living room.

'So how are you doing?' she asks as I reach down to grab the side of the sofa.

'Good, I guess.' I give a glance over my shoulder to the kitchen before I raise my side of the sofa up, intentionally bearing most of the weight because, like Callie, Liz is short and slender. But she seems to hold her own as she lifts her side up with almost the same ease as me.

'Just good?' she asks as she spins us in the opposite direction.

I shrug, letting out a loud exhale as we set the sofa down. 'It's been fun visiting you guys.'

She wipes the sweat from her brow. 'I don't mean with this trip,' she says. 'I mean this thing with your mom and dad.'

I'm not sure how to respond and thankfully, I don't have to because Dylan comes walking into the living room. He's got his phone in his hand and covering the receiver. 'Um . . .' he struggles, 'she wants to talk to you.'

He doesn't have to say who *she* is. I know it's my mother and I jerk back like he hit me. 'N-no,' I stammer weakly. 'I don't want to talk to her.'

He looks torn by how to reply, but I think it's because

arguing with my mom is the worst thing possible since, in her eyes, she's always right. 'Um . . .'

'Dylan, you shouldn't even ask him,' Liz hisses. 'Just tell her no.'

Dylan blinks like he snapped out of a trance then quickly puts the phone to his ear. 'He's not going to talk to you.'

I'm not sure what she says to him, but his shoulders look heavier with each second that ticks by. When he finally hangs up, he looks like a hunched over old man as he slumps onto the sofa Liz and I just moved. He lowers his head into his hands and presses his palms to his eyes.

'What did the evil bitch want now?' Liz asks, sitting behind Dylan. I decide right then and there that I like Liz.

'She wanted to tell us that' – he lifts his head and looks at me – 'Dad's probably not going to make it through the next week.' He presses his lips together and I can't tell whether he's upset about Dad or having to talk to Mom. 'She wants us to go to North Carolina and say our goodbyes.'

I swiftly shake my head, flexing my fingers, fighting the urge to pierce my nails into my flesh. 'No, I can't do that.'

'I know you can't.' His expression softens. 'And that's exactly what I told her.'

My muscles untense slightly. 'What about you? Are you . . . going to?'

Liz looks about as eager to hear his answer as I do.

'No,' he says firmly. 'I said my goodbyes the day I turned eighteen.'

Shutting my eyes, I nod. I feel like I'm on the verge of crying, thinking about how I never did get to say goodbye. That the last real exchange my father and I had was when he looked down at me with hateful eyes as I bled out on the kitchen floor. I wonder if he thought I was going to die. I wonder if he was happy because of it. I want to stop wondering about all this. I want to say goodbye like Dylan did, but not to my dad – to the past. And I want to go to my future.

'I need to go home.' I don't mean to say it aloud, but the moment I do is the moment I realize just how much I need it.

Thankfully, Dylan sees it, too, because he stands up and crosses the room, giving me a weird, awkward, but welcome hug. 'I know you do. And I think I have an idea.'

Chapter 21

#162 Have a Mad, Crazy Snowball Fight.

Callie

Before Jackson and I head to Laramie, he and my dad loaded up the truck with some furniture my mom decided to give me that was in the guestroom – the one that still isn't finished. It consists of a queen-size bedframe and mattress, a dresser and nightstand, along with a couple of barstools for the kitchen. She also threw in some of her old cooking supplies even though I told her I don't like to cook. I think I actually broke her heart when I said that, but so did me leaving earlier. She cried the entire time she was hugging me goodbye and then while Jackson and I were pulling out of the driveway.

'Thank God that's over,' Jackson remarks as he drives

toward Laramie. He'll only be there for two days, but he keeps insisting we're going to '*snowboard like pros and party like rock stars*' while we're there.

'She means well,' I say, taking my laptop out of a bag to get some work done for my internship, as I haven't done anything since Thanksgiving break started.

'She may *mean* well,' he says, pulling into a gas station so he can fill up the tank before we hit the highway, 'but she comes off crazy.'

I laugh, but don't go too much further into the making-fun-of-Mom. She may be a little intense, but deep down I do believe she means well and that her overbearing attitude lately is coming from what happened to me. I think she feels she needs to make up for it by smothering me, so instead of fighting her, I've decided to let her be. Of course, telling my brother this will only get me teasing remarks at being a mama's girl.

When Jackson gets out to put gas in the truck, I get in the backseat with my laptop on my lap. But even when he gets back in and starts driving again, I'm still staring at that damn cursor and I swear it's begging me to write something else. So even though I know I shouldn't, I switch to my fiction-yet-kind-of-non-fiction story and suddenly my fingers come alive.

This monster wasn't in disguise like the one she'd met so many years ago. He snarled his fangs and raised his fists, ready to break everything in his path.

Knowing that she would only get one chance with this, the girl rushed forward before she could back out.

'Stop.' Her voice was as small as she felt, and when the monster turned to look at her, she wanted to run. But honestly, she was sick of running, so tired of monsters winning.

'Can I help you?' the monster asked, his fangs disappearing, his eyes softening as he shape-shifted into his misleading form. He thought the girl couldn't see anymore what lay beneath the disguise, but she could.

The monster.

In his eyes.

'You're needed inside,' the girl lied, her voice surprisingly steady and her feet firmly planted on the ground. She glanced at the boy, who was standing so still she thought he might be frozen.

The monster looked back at the boy, too, and she couldn't see his eyes anymore, but by the way the boy cowered, she knew the man had shown the boy a glimpse of the monster waiting for him when she left.

When the man turned back to the girl, his disguise was back up as he smiled and nodded before he started inside. The girl held her breath as he walked by, afraid the monster might jump out and attack her.

He never did.

He must save it for the boy, *she thought sadly.*

Once the monster was in his palace, which looked more like a dungeon hidden beneath fancy walls, tall towers, and bright lights, she finally faced the boy.

'*Are you okay?' she asked tentatively. It'd been forever since the girl had spoken to a boy – to anyone, really – and she was nervous.*

'*I'm fine,' the boy said, the iciness in his tone startling her. Maybe she'd been wrong. Maybe the boy really couldn't see the monster living inside the man.*

'*O-okay.' Her voice quivered as she lowered her head and turned to go back home and back though the vines that surrounded her own torturous palace.*

'*Wait,' the boy called out before she could get too far.*

The sound of his voice calmed her, and when she faced him again, she was almost smiling for the very first time in six years.

The boy kept his distance, as if he feared the girl and was afraid to get to close. But that was okay; she feared his closeness as well.

'*Why did you do that?' he asked, wrapping his arms around himself.*

'Because . . .' She considered what to tell him. The truth? It seemed too terrifying to utter her secrets aloud. Maybe she could be vague, though. 'No one ever did it for me.'

'You know a monster, too?' the boy asked, and this time he took a step toward her.

The girl was afraid.

But she was also curious.

So she stayed.

'Yes,' she said, 'I do.'

'Does he . . . hurt you?'

She wanted to run, but found herself nodding. 'He did.'

The boy seemed sad and in pain as he moved toward her again, this time more quickly and with his hand stretched out. 'I'm sorry that he did.'

The girl looked at his hand, unsure what to do. She was afraid to touch him, afraid the boy could be wearing his own disguise and that suddenly a monster would appear in his place.

The boy must have read her mind because he pulled away and wrapped his arms around himself again. 'Thank you,' he uttered softly.

'For what?'

'For scaring him away.'

Again, the girl almost smiled and she could have sworn the boy did, too.

'You're welcome,' she replied, then the two of them stood there in the darkness, the distant lights from the castles seeming far away, but for the first time within reach.

I end up writing until my fingers ache and my eyes and brain feel like they're bleeding. It's the most tiring and satisfying feeling ever. By the time I'm getting out of the backseat to show Jackson my apartment, I feel high and can't help but think, *This is what I want forever. Just my computer, my tiny little apartment, and Kayden. I just wish I had him here with me right now.*

'So, who were you talking to on the phone the whole drive?' I ask Jackson as we trudge up the stairway. It's around noon, but the stormy sky makes it seem like it's much later, along with the quiet of the apartment complex.

He shrugs, scratching at the back of his neck. 'No one.'

'It was your girlfriend, huh?' I tease as I take my keys out of my bag.

He gapes at me. 'How'd you know?'

'Because of the way your voice sounded. All swoony.' I clasp my hands together and make my best swoony impression. Jackson actually blushes and it's so funny that I bust up laughing. 'Oh my God. I can't believe I'm just learning about her.' I find the right key on the chain as we reach the door. 'Do Mom and Dad know?'

'No,' he says quickly. 'And I'd prefer it if you didn't say anything for now. I've just started seeing her and I don't want Mom to get too attached to the idea yet, considering how she is with that stuff.'

'That doesn't seem fair for me to do that, considering how much you teased me about Kayden in front of them the entire week.' I stick the key in the lock and turn it, excited to be home.

'Callie, please,' he begs, which he never does.

It's super funny, but I decide to be nice. 'Fine. Mum's the word.' I push open the door and step back to let him in. 'But lay off on the teasing me, okay?'

He nods as he steps inside.

'So, this is where you live?' my brother states as he makes a small circle around the living room. There's not much to look at; a small suede couch we bought at a second-hand store, along with an entertainment center, and a brand-new television – that was the splurge. 'It's a good thing Mom let you bring all that shit with us, huh?'

I breathe in that fresh home scent as I shut the door behind me. 'Yeah, it was really nice of her.'

'I'm just trying to figure out how we're going to get all that furniture up here.' Jackson glances at the window as he rubs his jawline. The window is webbed with frost and snowflakes are splattered against it. 'Because the tarp's not going to hold up if it keeps snowing like this and there's no way I can carry it up here with you and your tiny little arms.'

I pull a face, but then it go because he's kind of right. 'It's been a really rough winter, hasn't it?' I plop down on the couch with the phone in my hand.

'I wouldn't know, since I live in sunny, awesome Florida.' Jackson grins conceitedly as he sits down on the armrest. 'When's Kayden supposed to be here? He and I could probably get all that shit up the stairs. I'm just super fucking relieved you're not on the third floor, although you should have picked the first floor.'

'Kayden's not going to be here until Monday evening,' I tell him, opening my contacts to text Luke because he's the only other strong guy I know. 'And I didn't pick the floor. Or the apartment really.'

He raises his eyebrows at me as he stuffs his hands into the pockets of his tan cargo pants. 'What do you mean?'

'I mean, Kayden picked this place out with Seth,' I say with a shrug. 'As a surprise for me.'

'But he knew you wanted to move in with him, right? He didn't just do it assuming?' He almost seems like he's asking for knowledge for himself, like maybe he's thinking about doing it with his girlfriend or something.

'Of course he knew I wanted to. I'd asked him a couple of weeks before then and he said he'd think about it, but then he surprised me with this.' I gesture around at my palace proudly, even though Jackson looks unimpressed. But I don't care. This is my palace and unlike the one in the story I'm writing, it doesn't have vines and thorns, but warmth and promises of happiness.

He gives me this strange look that I can't decipher. 'What?' I ask.

He shrugs. 'It's nothing.'

'It is something, otherwise you wouldn't be looking at me like a weirdo.'

That gets him to laugh. 'It really is nothing. I was just thinking about how you seem happy.' His shoulders keep lifting and falling. 'It's nice, and you deserve it.'

'Thanks, Jackson.' I smile at him as I text Luke to see if he can come help.

'Although, I have to say, I wouldn't tell Mom that whole story of him surprising you,' Jackson says. 'She'll think you're getting engaged.' He pauses then smirks at me. 'Though I wouldn't be surprised if you did at the rate you two are going.'

'Okay, *Mom*.' I roll my eyes at him then laugh, but Jackson doesn't join in.

'Just giving you a heads-up,' he tells me with a nonchalant lift of his shoulders. 'You seem kind of clueless with this stuff.'

I'd be offended, but I'm too distracted by the other thing he said. Is that where Kayden and I are heading? Why have I never thought of this?

I probably would have sat there all day, stuck in my head, if my phone didn't start going nuts in my hand.

Luke: Yeah, headed over. I'm not at my place, though, so it'll take me just a little bit longer.

Me: K, thanks. I owe u one :)

I put my phone away then get to my feet. 'I got you some non-tiny backup.'

My brother looks at me like I've lost my mind. 'What the hell are you talking about?'

'Luke's coming over to help you move the heavy stuff in,' I say, opening the front door. 'But while we wait, this tiny little girl with her tiny little arms is going to go bring up what she can because she's not as weak as she looks.'

'I know that, Callie.' My brother follows me outside and down the stairway. 'You're tougher than a lot of people.'

'Wow, two compliments in a day,' I joke, jumping off the last step and into a fluffy pile of snow that reaches the ankles of my boots. 'It's a miracle.'

'It'll be a miracle if it stopped snowing.' He zips his coat up to his chin and glares at the cloudy sky. 'I'm going to freeze my ass off.'

'The weather in Florida's making you kind of a baby.' I pick up a handful of snow and ball it up in my hand. 'You know that.'

Now he's glaring at me. 'You throw that at me and you're going to pay.'

I make the snow in my hand into a firm ball then I back down the frozen sidewalk. 'I'll only pay if you can catch me, but I have a feeling that Florida Boy is going to fail epically when I run up the snowbank.' Then I stick out my tongue and launch the snowball at him.

I don't think he thought I had the guts to do it because he doesn't even duck. It hits him straight in the face and I feel kind of bad, but not enough to stop myself from laughing.

Looking pissed off, he wipes the snow from his face with the sleeve of his jacket. 'You're so going to pay for that.' He cracks his knuckles as he walks toward me. 'I think you've forgotten how good I used to be at mad, crazy snowball fighting.'

'The key words being *used to*.' I take off running before I even finish my sentence, knowing full well that this is probably going to end with me getting my face shoved in the snow. He used to do it all the time when we were younger and Jackson hasn't grown up enough not to do it now.

Just like I predicted, by the end of our mad, crazy snowball fight, Jackson is smashing snow in my face. I'm on my back on the snowbank near the dumpster, laughing my butt off as he stands over me, pressing snow into my face. Out of the corner of my eye, I see Luke's truck pull up and park under the carport near the building.

'Fine, I give up!' I laugh, kicking at Jackson, feeling like a kid again, having fun with my older brother, something that stopped happening when I was twelve. 'Just stop! Luke's here.'

'I warned you not to mess with me.' His cheeks are red because I did manage to throw a few more snow-balls at his face. Just to be an ass, Jackson drops a handful of snow on the top of my head before helping me to my feet. Then we slip down the steep hill and walk back toward the carport area. My coat is full of snow and I try to shake it out while Jackson laughs his head off at me.

'This is so cold,' I say as we approach Luke's truck.

'Just wait until we hit the slopes,' Jackson replies, plucking some flakes of snow out of his hair. 'You're probably going to get a face full of snow every time you try to stop.'

My nose scrunches. 'Way to boost my confidence.'

Jackson's mouth spreads to a grin. 'Anytime.'

I'm thinking of a comeback when the truck door swings open and Luke hops out. He's wearing a vintage-looking leather coat, a beanie, and has black work boots on. 'Figures it has to be snowing when we do this,' he remarks, slipping a pair of gloves on.

Luke used to scare me when I first met him. He just has that look about him that screams 'back the heck off'. But once I got to know him, I realized he was actually really nice and that the look came from his own inner demons.

'I hope you don't mind, but I brought some people with me.' Right as he says it, Violet climbs out of the passenger side. Like Luke, she's wearing a beanie over her wild locks of red and black hair, boots, and a leather jacket, only unlike Luke, hers has studs in it. Violet is actually the perfect match for Luke and not just when it comes to looks, either. Although I can seriously picture two figurine replicas of them standing upon the top of a gothic wedding cake.

'The more the merrier,' Jackson tells Luke, stomping some snow off his boots. 'And the less I have to carry.'

'Well, aren't you just a gentleman,' Violet says sarcastically to my brother, unimpressed.

My brother responds by checking her out, his eyes quickly scrolling up her body.

I jab him in the side with my elbow. 'Ew, stop it,' I hiss under my breath. 'She's Luke's girlfriend and you have your own, remember?'

Jackson gives me a *whoops* look, totally busted. 'Sorry.'

I'm surprised by how easy he lets it go and I turn to Luke and Violet, reaching into my coat pocket to get my own gloves. 'Ready to get this party started?'

'Yeah, just as soon as I bundle up.' The voice doesn't come from either of them or my brother, but from the passenger side of the truck.

My head snaps in that direction, my heart leaping in my chest before I even see him. 'What the heck are you doing here?' I ask as I sprint around the back of the truck, nearly wiping out on a patch of ice, but I regain my footing and launch myself into Kayden's strong arms, a little too forcefully because he lets out a grunt.

His arms slip around me and he holds me tightly against him. 'I couldn't take it anymore. I needed to be here with you.'

'I needed you here, too,' I say, because even though I handled the thing with Caleb just fine, I'd needed him, something I'm discovering now.

'I know.' He hugs me tighter.

To everyone else, it probably looks like we're happily reuniting. That, like the apartment, this was another amazing surprise. And it is in a way. But only I can hear the desperation in Kayden's voice, the silent plea for me to never let him go.

And it's exactly what I do.

Chapter 22

#164 Party Dance Like a Rock Star.

Kayden

Dylan had let me use his flyer miles to change flights and go home early, but only if I promised to visit for Christmas and bring Callie. Hopefully, Callie won't mind that I agreed because I really just wanted to go home to her.

The flight home, I'm a mess and have to keep repeating to myself all the reasons why I don't need to cut.

Callie.

I don't want to go back to that place where I become that person again.

I'm not happier when I do it.

It's unhealthy, both mentally and physically.

219

Callie.

I'll have to start all over again.

My body already has too many scars.

I want to be better.

I need to let go of the past.

Callie.

Callie.

Callie.

That list streams through my head for the entire trip and it keeps me intact and clearly shows what is important to me. By the time I make it to the apartment – to Callie – I'm an emotional wreck, but in a good way.

I don't really get to talk to Callie very much for the rest of the day, though I'm desperate to. We spend most of the afternoon unloading the truck, then take a break in the living room before heading out to get something to eat because everyone is 'starving to death'.

'You need some pictures on your wall,' Jackson says, sitting down on the sofa and glancing around at our bare white walls. He takes off the beanie he's wearing and tosses it aside. 'It'd make this place look better.'

'We'll get there,' Callie replies, plopping down on the barstool next to the one I'm sitting on. Luke and Violet are sprawled out on the floor, cheeks red and looking as exhausted as I feel. There are pieces of furniture and boxes everywhere, but it feels like we've made progress toward turning this place into a home. 'I'm still working on getting some up.'

'I don't think we have any,' I say, picking at the label on my water bottle. 'At least not any of you and me.'

'You don't think I've taken pictures of you,' she says, pressing her hand to her chest, feigning being offended.

I manage to peel the damp label off and set it on the counter. 'You have some of me?'

'Of us.' She nudges me with her elbow and smiles. But when I don't return it, she falters. 'What's wrong?'

'It's nothing.' I shrug and say in a low voice so no one else can hear me, 'It's just, pictures on a wall? Is that what people do, because we sure as hell didn't, growing up.' But I can't help thinking of Dylan's place and all the pictures they have up on the wall – a life, and a good one. Is that where I'm heading? Can I have that?

It's crazy that I don't have to say it, that she can actually see what I'm thinking. 'It'll make this place not just an apartment, but a home.' She leans over and gives me a peck on the lips.

I'm about to pull her in for a deeper kiss, but Jackson clears his throat. 'Okay, I say it's time to get some grub.'

221

Callie sighs against my lips. 'We'll talk later.'

I nod and then we all head out and pile into Callie's dad's car, which is roomier than my car, and Luke's truck. Luke manages to turn up some classic rock that everyone pretends they don't know but ends up belting out the lyrics. By the time we hit up a local, mellower bar in town, everyone is laughing, in a good mood, but so exhausted that it takes us forever to make it inside.

'So much for partying like a rock star,' Callie jokes to Jackson as we settle into a booth. There's some alternative music playing in the background and a few people dancing. 'You must be so disappointed in me.'

Jackson reaches for a menu tucked between the salt shakers. 'Nah, I'm kind of tired myself.' He flips open the menu. 'Must be getting old.'

'You better watch it,' she teases. 'You're one step away from sitting around in your sweat pants on weekends and yelling at the television when your team fumbles the ball.'

'Hey, I do that sometimes,' I intervene. 'Well, minus the sweatpants.' I flash her a flirty grin and wink. 'I just do it naked.'

'Glad to know what I have to look forward to,'

Callie says, then winks back at me. It makes me laugh for the first time since I've gotten back from Virginia.

'Good God, please don't go there,' Jackson mutters with all his attention on the menu. 'I really don't want to hear about what my sister and her boyfriend do behind closed doors.'

'Sorry, man.' I actually used to hate Jackson for the way he treated Callie and for bringing Caleb into her life. I still carry a little disdain for him, but Callie seems to have let it go, so I'm trying to be nice. But I want to talk to Callie openly without her brother listening, so I slide to get out of the booth, Luke giving me a begrudging huff of frustration when he has to get out of my way.

'Where are you going?' Callie asks as I stand up and stretch my arms above my head, constraining a grin when I notice her checking out the sliver of my stomach that peeks out from the bottom of my red shirt.

'To dance.' I nod my chin in the direction of the dance area. 'Want to come?'

She shakes her head. 'Nah, I kind of want to see you shaking your thing solo.' When I start to frown, she laughs. 'Of course I'll join you, silly boy.' She's sitting between Violet and her brother, and motions for Violet to let her out.

Once she's on her feet, she laces her fingers through mine and pulls me toward the dance floor where couples are grinding on each other. She's wearing black skinny jeans tucked in lace-up boots along with a red shirt. Her hair is up and the only makeup she has on is some black liner. She's probably the most dressed woman here and the most beautiful.

When we reach the center of the floor, I pull her to me and she rests her head on my chest as we start swaying to the beat of 'Ho Hey' by The Lumineers.

'So why'd you really come home early?' she asks so softly I can barely hear her over the music.

'Because I wanted to make sure you were okay.' I press my hand to her lower back, the other on her hips as I rest my chin on the top of her head.

'But there's more to it than that.' It's not a question, but a statement.

My initial reaction is to lie, but then I realize I don't want to lie to her anymore, don't want to be that guy. 'Because I wasn't handling things well.'

Her hands tighten around the back of my neck, pulling me closer to her. 'Did you—'

'No,' I cut her off so she doesn't have to ask. 'I wanted to, though. Things were already hard when I learned about my father and about what happened with Caleb, but then it got worse when my mother called and wanted to talk to me.'

Her hold on me tightens. 'Did you talk to her?'

'No . . . I couldn't.'

'Good. I'm glad. You shouldn't. Not until we know where she stands. And maybe not even then.'

'I love you,' I say because it's all I can say at the moment. The way she's always protecting me, it's too much sometimes to even comprehend.

She leans back to look me in the eyes. 'I don't think you should ever even consider talking to her again unless you want to, no matter what happens.'

'I won't,' I say. 'Although I was kind of curious what she had to say . . . probably something bad, but still she's . . .'

'She's your mom and you feel like you have to talk to her,' Callie finishes for me. 'But she needs to start acting like a mother before you treat her like one.'

'I'm not sure I ever want to, anyway.'

'Then don't. You don't owe her anything.'

Her words are exactly what I need to hear, and I no longer want to dwell on family stuff. I want desperately to let go of it, so I change the subject. 'You and your brother seem to be getting along.'

She shrugs, staring up at me with those beautiful

eyes of hers. 'It's been nice hanging out with him.'

'Good. I'm glad. It's nice to see you happy around your family.'

'My mom wants *us* to come visit,' she says, emphasizing her point that I'm included in this.

'Dylan wants *us* to do the same thing,' I say, mimicking her emphasis.

It gets her to laugh, her eyes crinkling at the corners. 'Families are needy, aren't they?' As soon as she says it, she looks worried, like she's offended me or something.

'Callie, you don't have to be careful with me. You can say the word family and I'll be fine.' I catch her gaze flick to my wrists, which I'm proud to say are free of any fresh cuts. 'And besides, I'm learning that family doesn't always mean what I thought it did. Dylan and his wife are nice, and Tyler wasn't a dick.' Keeping one hand on her back, I put the other on her cheek. 'But honestly, you're more of my family than anyone else. All I need is you and me and our tiny little apartment, and I'm good. I realized that while I was in Virginia.'

She swallows hard, her eyes welling up, but she looks happy not sad. 'Good, because it's all I need, too.' Then she stands up on her tiptoes and plants a soft kiss on my mouth. 'From now on,' she whispers against my lips, 'we take all trips and vacations together.'

'Deal,' I say then coax her lips apart with my tongue so I can kiss her as deeply as I want.

We keep moving and kissing until the song ends. When it switches to a faster-tempo one, I decide to step up my skills. Like the first time we danced, I slide my hand down her arm, push her out then spin her around until she crashes into my chest.

She busts up laughing, throwing her head back. 'You know, we may not have gotten to party like rock stars, but we sure as heck can dance like them.'

'We sure as hell can,' I say, spinning her around and around until she's laughing so hard she's crying. 'We can do anything – you and me – when we're together.'

Her laughing silences as she stares up at me. 'I want this . . . you and me . . . forever.'

I wet my lips with my tongue, noting how much my heart accelerates, noticing how much I don't want to run.

Stay.

Stay.

Stay.

My heart beats.

Forever.

And ever.

And ever.

'Me, too,' I say, then kiss her with as much passion as my heart is carrying, letting her know just how much I love her, and that I always will.

Chapter 23

#165 Accept the Phone Call You've Been Dreading.

Kayden

A week passes without anything major happening, and I think, Maybe my life is finally going to get some normalcy. My days consist of practice, school, Callie, work, Callie, and practice. I love the routine and it starts to get me wondering if maybe Dylan was right, perhaps it's time to let everything with my father go. Move on. Accept football might be my thing and just own it. It doesn't need to be associated with my father if *I* don't want it to be.

Yep, everything is going great in that thing we call life until I got that goddamn call.

The thing is, I knew it was coming, knew it would happen eventually. But what I wasn't prepared for was who would deliver the news to me. Maybe if I did, I could have prepared myself more.

The unknown number should have been a red flag, but I was working on a final paper and so I was a little distracted when I answered it.

God, I wish I hadn't been distracted.

'Your father's dead.' The sound of my mother's voice almost sidetracks me from what she said.

'How the fuck did you get my number?' I shove the textbooks out of the way and sit up in bed. 'Did Dylan give it to you?' If so, then I'm super pissed. And hurt.

She lets out a hollow laugh. 'Yeah, right. Like he would ever do that. He thinks he's protecting you from us by keeping us disconnected.'

I relax a little, relieved Dylan didn't betray me. And I'm a little pissed off at myself for instantly jumping to that conclusion. 'He is, though.'

'Well, you can believe what you want,' she says, her icy tone unsettlingly familiar. 'But people shouldn't disown their family.'

'I didn't disown you. You chose to leave and I chose not to let you back in.' I swing my legs over the edge of the bed, putting my feet on the floor. 'And I've been doing fine with that choice – better than I have my entire life.'

230

'Well, I'm sorry we make you so miserable.' She sounds anything but sorry. Irritated, yes. Sorry, no. There's a pause and I think she's waiting for me to disagree with her statement, but I'm not going to. 'Well, anyway. I thought I'd call to let you know you're now officially fatherless.'

'Okay.' Again, I feel nothing.

Nothing.

Empty.

Cold.

Without a heart.

Except I do have a heart.

It just beats for someone else.

For people who deserve it.

Callie.

'Jesus, Kayden, you could at least pretend to sound upset about it,' she says in a surprisingly even tone for someone who just lost her husband.

'Yeah, well, I guess I'm not as good at pretending as you are.' I lower my head into my hand, wanting to take what I said back because it's rude and spiteful, and I don't want to be that. But I can't bring myself to retract what I'm really feeling and *pretend*.

'I can't believe how you're acting,' she snaps. 'I raised you to be better than this. Raised you to be the kind of person that would at least come say goodbye to their father before he passed. You know how weird it looked to the doctors and nurses for none of his children to show up?' My mother has always been into appearances, her motto being that as long as everyone thinks everything is perfect, then it is.

'About as bad as it looked for the entire town when I got arrested, I'm sure. Or when I was committed because of my cutting.'

'I can't believe you're bringing that up.'

'And I can't believe you called me.' I get up from the bed and start pacing the room, trying to channel my adrenaline in the healthiest way I can think of. *I will not give in. I won't.* 'Dylan could have given me the update.'

'Update? I can't believe you just called your father's death an update.' She's verging toward crying. I should feel bad, but I can't find the will to bring that emotion out of me for her. 'After everything he did for you; put you into sports, put a roof over your head, bought you all the things you needed.'

'There's so much more to life than materialism, Mother. And so much more to being a parent than buying your children the shit they need, like, say, loving them and not beating them up or stabbing them.'

'I didn't do any of those things.' She tries to sound calm, but I can tell she's crying, almost losing it completely, which is something I've never seen or heard her do before.

I should stop.

I should care enough to stop.

But I don't.

'No, you just let it happen,' I say through gritted teeth, 'which is just as bad.'

'We are not bad parents!' she cries hysterically, shocking me because I honestly didn't think she possessed emotion. 'We're not . . .' The last part sounds like she's trying to convince herself, not me.

I can't take it anymore. Bad mother or not, I don't want to be the kind of person to bring others pain. Don't want to be like them. Don't want to carry this heaviness in me anymore. I want to let it go – be free. So I make a choice, one that will hopefully set me free.

'I'm sorry.'

'For what?'

'For saying all those things . . .' *Even though they're true.*

'Good. Now, let's talk about your father's funeral and what you can help me with.'

I stop pacing. 'No.'

'What?' She sounds shocked.

'I'm not helping you with any of that.'

'But he's your father . . .' That's the best argument she can come up with and it's sad. 'And you just said you were sorry.'

'Yeah, for saying hateful things,' I say, breathing through the pain tearing at my chest, through the tears starting to fall. I'm letting go – accepting what is. I can feel myself on the edge of it. But the thing is, I'm letting go of a lot and I'm worried I'm going to explode when I finally say goodbye to it all – the hate, the pain, the resentment. 'But not for feeling the way that I do. I'll never be sorry for that, nor will I help with his funeral.'

'So you're not coming.' She's still crying, but she sounds angry.

'I might, but I'm not sure yet.' I stand up and grab my car keys and jacket before heading out of the room. 'You can give Dylan the details and then he can pass them along to me.'

'You're a terrible son.'

The only things that keep me from listing off the terrible things she is, are 1) She's hurting and even though I despise her, I don't want to be that person.

234

And 2) It doesn't matter; she's my past if I choose to let her be.

And I think I do.

'That's your opinion' – I jerk open the front door, telling myself to keep breathing, to keep doing what I'm doing. Moving forward . . . move forward . . . one step at a time – 'and I can live with that.' I make another choice and hang up, not giving her any more room to insult me or make me angry.

I head for my car and then in the direction of quite possibly the best choice I have ever made.

Chapter 24

#166 Hold Someone While They Let it All Out.

Callie

We finish up the Thanksgiving break by snowboarding and going out before Jackson returns home. Then Kayden and I get to spend some time together – finally – in our new home.

I still visit Harper a couple of times to make sure everything's going okay with therapy. She seems a little less fake and a bit more real, so when she tells me it's going good, I believe her. It makes me happy that I got to help her with that, almost as if it was a healing process I didn't even know about.

School goes on. Football goes on. Writing goes on. Life goes on. The next week goes by pretty uneventful. But the thing that Kayden and I both knew was coming finally arrives, smack dab in the middle of finals. I'm actually finishing up a test in Oceanography when I get a call from Kayden. I only know it's him because of the ringtone, but I can't answer it if I don't want to get accused of cheating.

I hurry and finish up the last of the questions then grab my bag and rush out of the classroom, tossing the exam on the teacher's desk as I go by. As soon as I'm out into the fairly empty hallway, I dig my phone out of my pocket and call him back.

'Hey, what's up?' I ask when he answers it.

He takes a deep breath and immediately I know whatever he called for has to be bad. 'It's my dad. He's dead.'

'I'll be right there,' I say, practically running toward the exit doors at the end of the hallway. All I can picture is him locked in the bathroom with a razor in his hand. 'Are you at home?'

'No, I'm actually in the parking lot.' Emotion surfaces through his voice, cracking down the line, and I swear I can actually feel it. 'I needed to see you so I've been sitting out here waiting for you to get out of class.'

'I'm coming.' I burst out the doors and sprint across the snow, grasping onto my bag. 'Where are you parked exactly?'

'At the front.' There's a vulnerability to his voice, like he's fighting not to break apart before I get there.

I scan the parking lot and when I spot his car, I veer right, not slowing down until I reach it. I throw open the door and jump in. He's sitting in the driver's seat, staring ahead at the campus quad, his jaw set tight, as his chest rises and crashes. He has on his pajama pants and a hoodie, which means he probably left the house in a hurry.

The warm air kisses my skin, but the silence of him chills my heart. I'm not sure what to say – if there's anything I can say. What the heck does one say to someone in this type of situation?

I'm sorry.

That you lost your dad.

Lost the monster in your life.

That you're hurting.

That you're confused.

That you have to go through this.

'I love you.' It's all I can think of and it seems to be exactly what he needs to hear because he turns to me, eyes soft as he leans over and wraps his arms around me, pulling me to him. My stomach presses into the console, but I still give in as he hugs me closer, almost in desperation.

'I love you, too,' he whispers with his head buried in my neck. 'God, I fucking love you. And really, that's all that matters.' I can feel the exact moment when he starts to cry, not because I can feel his tears or even hear him. I can feel it because of how tight his hold on me gets, like every one of his muscles is forcing the emotion out of him.

I wrap my arms around him and run my fingers through his hair, remaining quiet while he cries because there's not much more I can do. He needs to get it out and I'm glad he is. It's when he holds it in that things become a problem.

I'm not even sure how long we sit there like that, well into the evening, but I don't dare move, afraid he'll suck all the emotion back inside himself and trap it there.

By the time he pulls away, the sky has cleared, but the sun is lowering behind the mountains, casting its orange neon glow against the snow on the ground. There are hardly any people left on campus and the parking lot is nearly vacant.

'Are you okay?' I ask as he wipes his bloodshot eyes with the back of his hand.

'Yeah, sorry about that.' His voice is hoarse. 'I just lost it for a second.'

239

'You know, it's okay to lose it,' I say, reaching over to wipe away a few tears remaining. I'm about to pull away when he leans into my touch so I keep my hand there. 'And it's okay to cry.'

'I know it is,' he says, letting out a heavy exhale. 'And I think I needed to do it – let it all out. I've needed to for the last twenty years.'

There's a pause and I'm about to ask if he wants to talk about it when he leans back in the seat, facing forward then puts the car into reverse. 'I know you have questions,' he says as I buckle my seatbelt. 'And I'll answer them, but I just want to be home when I do, if that's okay?'

I nod, turning forward in my own seat. 'Of course that's okay.'

He looks relieved as he pulls out of the parking lot and onto the street. On our way back to the apartment, we stop to pick up some takeout because neither one of us is great at – nor do we enjoy – cooking. Then we settle on the sofa with our hamburgers, fries, and drinks, and eat in silence even though it just about drives me crazy.

'It was my mother who called,' he finally says as he picks up his drink and fiddles with his straw. 'She found out my number and called to tell me herself.'

'Was she . . .?' I pick at my hamburger. 'Was she nice?'

He shakes his head as he takes a sip of his drink. 'No, she was exactly herself.'

Okay, now I'm really worried. 'Kayden, I—'

He cuts me off by leaning forward and brushing his lips across mine. When he pulls away, he seems content. 'I'm fine, Callie. I promise.' As if to prove this point, he sets his food down and takes my hand in his. 'I got to tell her a lot of stuff I never had the balls to and then I realized that I was done.'

'Done?'

'With all of it. With her. With hating both of them. With letting them still affect my life even when they're not here.' He takes my food from my hand, sets it down on the coffee table, and scoots toward me until our knees touch. 'I'm going to let it go.' Determination pours from his eyes and overpowers me to the point I feel like I'm drowning in it – the pain he's releasing himself from. 'I'm going to focus on the future. Keep going to school and play my fucking heart out and hope I get drafted. And if I don't, I'll have my degree to fall back on.' He reaches for me, tucking strands of hair behind my ear, before placing his warm palm on my cheek. 'And I'm going to take care of you and make you so happy.' Emotion radiates through his eyes as his gaze steadily holds mine. 'I want to keep going down this path with you. I want us to have a future – you and me.'

Maybe Jackson was right. Maybe we are headed in the direction of marriage. God, what if we are? Do I want it?

I nod eagerly. 'I want that, too, more than anything else.' I pause, 'But . . .'

His brows knit, his confidence faltering a bit. 'But what?'

'But . . .' I hesitate again, nervous to bring it up. 'But what about the funeral? Are you . . .? Are you going to go to it?'

'I'm not sure yet.' He's not angry or sad, just confused.

'Well, either way, I support you.' I turn my head and delicately kiss his palm. 'I'm here for you if you want to go and say goodbye. Get some closure, maybe.'

His eyes are soft, his expression full of nothing but love. 'I know you are.' It's within that moment I think I realize that we're going to be okay. Sure, there'll probably be bumps down the road for us – there always will be when it comes to life – but he's finally letting me love him like he deserves and that's a huge, epic step for us.

Life-changing, even.

The rest of the night is relaxing, falling into our routine. We eat. We talk. Then after Kayden falls asleep in bed, I write.

I'm starting to love our routine.

As soon as my fingers hit the keys, they come alive, eager to write and be free.

After the girl saved the boy, they didn't see each other for many sunrises and sunsets. Not because they chose to, but because they'd gone their separate ways and done their separate things, which is the case most of the time in life.

The girl had moved out of her palace and found a new place to live — a new life for herself where she wasn't constantly haunted by the memories of the monster. She actually felt happier than she had in a long time, partly because she'd been able to leave her past behind, but also because the night she saved the boy, something changed inside her. She'd stood up to a monster and even though it wasn't her own, it made her feel braver and less fearful in a world that seemed so scary all the time.

And the boy . . . well, she didn't know what had become of the boy, if he'd escaped the monster or not, but she hoped so. Hoped he was moving on like her.

Hoped he found happiness in those sad eyes of his.

It was during a warm fall day that she found out what

he'd been doing. Their reuniting was anything but magical, but it was still momentous, a literal crashing-into when they just happened to be in the same place at the same time.

Smack.

They ran into each other head on, the impact intense, but not as intense as seeing each other again.

They were in shock.

Stunned.

Breathless.

But most of all, they were just glad to see each other alive and breathing.

'Hey,' the girl said as the wind and leaves danced around them.

'Hey,' the boy replied back, looking better than he had before. His eyes, although they still carried sadness, also carried happiness.

Their first words weren't the best of opening lines, not like in the fairytales the girl had read when she was a princess. Stories that promised fantasies of princes sweeping princesses off their feet, wooing hearts with words and sometimes song.

But that was okay.

She didn't need wooing.

She didn't need songs.

244

Because she wasn't a princess.

And the boy wasn't a prince.

She was just a girl.

And he was just a guy.

And this wasn't a fairytale.

But real life.

And fairytales were overrated anyway.

The rest of their conversation was light, cautious, neither of them comfortable enough to bring up that night. They soon parted ways, with a wave and a smile that carried hope they would soon see each other again.

It was not the end for these two.

There was so much more in store for them.

Now that their monsters were out of their lives.

It didn't start right away — the relationship between the two of them. They had a class together and their conversations were filled with, 'Can I borrow a pen?' and 'Did you go to my game on Friday?' and 'You should really go to my game.'

The girl wanted to say more and so did the guy, but it took some time just to work up the courage to take that extra step.

But finally the time came.

'So I was thinking,' the guy said one day when they'd run into each other in the hallway. He was standing up *straighter these days, more confident now that he wasn't being beaten down. 'That we should go out some time.'*

'Like on a date?' The girl had never been out on a date and she was confused. Yes, they'd talked a little bit to one another and she couldn't stop thinking about him – her journal was filled with pages of their average encounters and of course the details of his eyes because those were her favorite part – but other than that, they'd seemed like they were going to be friends, which was way better than not being friends. But now, his expression showed signs of something else, as if he'd been trying to fight it, but had given it up and let it free.

I like you, *his expression read.*

I like you, too, *the girl wanted to say.*

'Yeah, on a date.' He seemed amused by the girl, almost nonchalant about the whole thing, but his eyes promised, I like you a lot.

I like you a lot, too.

'Okay.' It was hard for the girl to say, and when the words left her lips, they surprised her.

They surprised the guy, too, as if he'd thought she was going to say no. If she didn't know any better, she could have sworn they both stood taller.

'Okay then,' the guy said. 'I'll pick you up tonight.'

'Okay.'

They parted ways, the girl's head swimming with possibilities.

But could she trust him?

Because in a world full of monsters, it was hard to tell who was what.

Chapter 25

#167 Say Goodbye.

Kayden

It's not until Dylan calls me the next day I decide to go to the funeral because he says he's going. Tyler's not, though, because he was worried it might send him back into a relapse, which I understand. I honestly keep waiting for something to set me off and do the same thing, but I feel strangely okay.

I think Callie's relieved when I tell her I'm going to the funeral, like she thinks it will give me a sense of closure. I'm not sure if she's right, but it's the only chance I'm going to get, so I take it.

The funeral is in North Carolina, where I just found out my mother grew up, which is why my father and she had been hiding out there — because they knew people. Callie comes with me, thankfully, but we can only stay for two days because finals are going on and there's no way I'm going to fuck up my grades or hers for this. With the limited time we have there, we mostly just hang out on the beach near our hotel.

And I'm okay with that.

In fact, it's perfect.

'I'm starting to become a fan of the ocean,' Callie says the morning of the funeral. She's sitting between my legs in the sand, leaning back against my chest, the sun beaming down on us. 'It's so peaceful.'

I'm playing with her hair as the water crashes against the shore just a few feet in front of us. 'Yeah it is.'

She rests her head against me and lets out a contented sigh. 'We should come here more often.' She adjusts her sunglasses over her eyes. 'Well, not to North Carolina, but to the ocean.'

'We could always live by the ocean,' I say, putting one arm around her and leaving the other in the sand to support our weight, 'after we graduate, and maybe I'll get lucky and get drafted to a team that's near the coast.'

'I love hearing you talking about your future.' She turns her head and nuzzles into me. 'It always worried me when you wouldn't.'

I run my fingers through her hair and brush it out of her eyes so I can see her face. 'I'm sorry it took me so long to get to that point, but I'm glad you waited for me.'

'You're worth the wait,' she says, breathing me in. Then she starts grinning in amusement, shaking her head at herself. 'You've also turned me into a walking romance novel, FYI.'

'I'm not sure what you mean?'

Leaning back, she draws down her sunglasses to look at me. 'I keep uttering these cheesy lines every time I'm around you. It's becoming ridiculous.'

I chuckle softly. 'I think it's cute.'

'Well, you do it, too,' she says, amused. 'All the time.'

I start to scrunch up my nose and protest, but then I realize she's right. So instead, I get to my feet, brush the sand off my hands, and throw her over my shoulder.

'Kayden, what the heck!' she cries through her laughter, pounding on my back as I rush toward the water and wade in until I'm waist deep. We're not in our swimsuits, but shorts, and the water is lukewarm, and still not comfortable. But it's fun.

'This is for turning me into a sap,' I tease, pinching her ass before I lower her into the water with a splash.

She lets out a squeal as the salty ocean seeps through

her clothes all the way up to just below her chest. 'You are a mean, mean boy.'

'No way. I'm a sappy guy, thanks to you.' I give her a lopsided grin as I grab the front of her shirt and pull her closer to me. Her hair is dripping wet, water beads her skin, and her clothes cling to her body. She's ridiculously sexy and I just want to lick the water right off her skin.

So I do.

Dipping my head toward her neck, I lick a path across her collarbone, ignoring the salty taste.

'Kayden,' she gasps, her fingers tangling through my hair.

She pulls me closer and I smile against her skin as I drop my head lower, my hands gliding up to her stomach. I kiss a path to the collar of her shirt then pull it down to suck on the curve of her breast. She struggles to stand upright against the intensity of the waves rolling toward us, so I reach down, grab her thigh, and hitch it around my hip. She gasps and rocks her hips against me, seeking more. The moment is perfect and I'm about to give our bodies everything they're craving when a large wave slams against us and knocks us apart.

'Holy shit.' I struggle to get my footing as Callie comes up from out of the water.

'Serves you right' – she laughs and swims toward shore – 'for throwing me in there to begin with,' she says as she crawls out of the water and drops down on the sand, exhausted.

I wade out and lie down beside her, completely unconcerned that the sand is getting caked to my clothes. Then we stare at the sky, getting lost in the peace of just being near each other. But it's when the clouds roll in that I'm reminded why we're here.

'We should probably get ready to go,' Callie whispers softly with her arm draped over her forehead.

I slowly nod. 'Yeah, you're probably right.' It takes me a minute to move, though, and in the end, I wish I could have stayed.

Just her and me.

Callie and me.

The warm sand.

The peaceful ocean.

That's all I want.

But deep down, I know it's time for me to go say goodbye.

Dylan and Liz show up at our hotel a few hours before the funeral to take us out for lunch. Callie's wearing a black dress that looks a lot like Liz's and Dylan and

I are wearing black pants, a white shirt, and a black tie. None of our moods seem as sullen as our outfits, though.

'I can't believe you're a writer,' Liz says to Callie from across the table at the fast food place we're eating at. 'That's so cool.'

Callie seems a little self-conscious with the attention focused solely on her. 'Yeah, I guess. But I still have a lot of stuff to do if I'm going to make writing my career.'

I drape my arm around her and comb my fingers through her hair that still has the faintest scent of the ocean. 'You *are* going to be one. It's what you love to do.'

She scrunches up her face. 'I just don't want to think of it as a job, you know. The internship is great and everything, but I don't know. It's just not as fun as writing stories.'

'You should write stories, then. If that's what you want to do,' I say, picking up a fry and popping it into my mouth.

'Easier said than done.' She dunks a fry into my cup of ranch. 'Do you know how hard of a career that is to get into?'

'You can do it,' I say with a smile. 'And I'll take

care of you while you do.' *I promised I'd take care of you*, I mouth.

'You guys are adorable,' Liz interrupts our little moment. When I look across the table, I realize she and my brother are watching us with fascination. 'Seriously, like the cutest thing I've ever seen.'

Dylan rolls his eyes. 'Don't worry. She thinks everything's adorable. Puppies, kittens, bedding, cars, movies, old people.' He flashes her a grin and she smiles, playfully swatting her hand against his chest.

'Oh, whatever,' she says. 'You get all misty-eyed during movies, too.'

He keeps grinning at her and she throws a fry at his face, but he opens his mouth and catches it. We're all having fun and I almost forget why we're here, until Liz gets up from the booth.

'It's time to go,' she tells everyone with a sigh as she glances at the clock on the wall.

This somber silence sets over us as we're forced back to reality and the real reason the four of us are here hanging out in North Carolina.

To say goodbye.

'I guess it is,' Dylan mutters as he gets up and heads for the door, fumbling to get the car keys from his pocket.

We all follow in silence and get into the car. The drive to the church doesn't seem long enough. I wish I could make it last forever. We ride with my brother, sitting in the backseat where I hold Callie's hand the entire way, which helps me to breathe easier. The air is humid, the ocean is the scenery for most of the way. It's calming, but I still feel my heart thumping deafeningly inside my chest the closer we get to the place.

This is it.

Can I handle it?

Finally, we arrive at the small, almost rundown-looking church that's centered in the middle of the small town with the cemetery on the same street. The parking lot hardly has any cars in it, which makes me wonder if we're at the right place. But I don't say anything, as Dylan seems positive this is where it is, since 'this is where the GPS took us'. When we're walking up the sidewalk, though, he grabs my arm and pulls me back, motioning at Callie and Liz to go ahead.

Liz and Callie give us both a strange look as they pause in front of the large doors.

'It's okay,' Dylan says at the same time I say, 'I'm fine.'

With reluctance, they both go inside, leaving Dylan

and me standing at the bottom of the stairs in the shadows of the trees.

'So, if things start to get too heavy in here, just say so and we'll go,' he says, fiddling around with the watch on his wrist. He seems as uneasy as I feel.

'Okay.' I glance up at the door and then back to him, realizing that once I step inside, things are going to change. A chapter in my life is going to be closed and however I feel about it, in the end I'm saying goodbye forever, like when Dylan left the house at eighteen. 'I have a question, though . . . about how Dad died . . .' I have no clue why I'm asking, other than it seems like I should know before I walk in there, before I say goodbye and close the chapter. 'Do you know what happened exactly that put him in the hospital?'

Dylan appears uncomfortable, apprehensively loosening his tie. 'I do, but are you sure you want to hear it?'

It takes me a beat to answer, but in the end it feels like I should know. 'Yeah, I think I need to, for closure.'

He sighs then rakes his hand through his hair, staring out at the parking lot. 'I don't know all the details, but it was a fight.'

Shock ripples through me and slams against my chest. 'What?'

Dylan sighs, looking back at me. 'He finally got into a fight with someone who fought back.' He shakes his head and then stares out at the large oak trees around the yard in front of the church. 'It's kind of tragic when you think about it. So much useless and unnecessary rage for all those years finally led him to the end. It was such a waste, to live life like that.'

'I know it was,' I say quietly. 'Being happy is so much better, isn't it?'

Nodding, Dylan looks at me and the edginess in his eyes has vanished and all that remains is pity. Not for me, but for our dad. 'It really, really is. Too bad he could never figure that out.'

Silence wraps around us, and even though we don't agree that it's time to go in, we both move for the door at the same time and enter the church. It's about as empty as the parking lot, with a few people sitting on the benches, faces I don't recognize except for one person who I knew would be there, and who I was dreading seeing.

My mother.

She's sitting at the front, dressed in black, with a hat on her head and a veil over her face. She turns her head when we enter, the hinges of the church door announcing our presence. We exchange this look. I don't know what

257

it means, nor do I care to find out. Because when she starts to get up, I rip my gaze away from her and sit down beside Callie because that's where I belong. I'm surprised that my mother takes the hint and sits back down, staring ahead at the coffin upfront. It looks so lonely up there with no flowers around it, no large photo to represent the man that he was.

Callie holds my hand the entire time. We don't say much, but there's not much to say. Besides, she's here with me and that's all that really matters – that she loves me enough to be here for me.

As the funeral goes on, the emptier the church feels with the lack of crying. There's no heart-warming eulogy dedicated to him. No one has anything to say.

There is only silence.

Emptiness.

Which is really what his life was, wasn't it?

It's in that moment that I feel sort of sorry for my dad. What a waste, to live life with so much anger that there's no room for love. I'm grateful I'm not like him. Grateful I have the chance to move on from all the pain and hate he inflicted in my life. Grateful I was capable of love. Grateful for Callie, my brother, Liz, Luke, Violet, Seth, Greyson, and even my coach. Because in the end, I realized I'm not my father.

I'm simply me.

And that's enough.

I wish I could have said that toward the end of his funeral when we took him to the cemetery to put him in his final resting place. To find it in my heart to say a few words that meant something.

But I couldn't.

All I could say was goodbye.

And let the past go.

Forever.

Chapter 26

#168 Try Not to Get Too Embarrassed in the Most Embarrassing Situation.

Callie

Ever since the funeral, Kayden seems to be doing a lot better. I don't ask him why because really it doesn't matter. All that does matter is the darkness that has always haunted him seems to have lifted. Don't get me wrong, he's not happy all the time, but no one is, really.

It's Christmas Day, which we're spending at my parents' house. We've been there for a few days now and plan to stay through New Year's. While I had suggested we go to Virginia, not only because I know that his brother wanted him to come out there, but because I knew my mother was going to act like a weirdo, he asked if we could go to my home. Plus, there was the fact that I was worried I'd run into Caleb again, but my mother assured me he was behind bars, awaiting his trial. And Kayden said it was fair that we came here, since I'd already spent time with his brother and sister. I didn't feel too good about it, though, since the time I spent with his brother and sister-in-law was at the funeral, but he promised me he really wanted to go visit my family.

Poor guy didn't know what he was in store for.

'I love Christmas,' my mother singsongs as she waltzes around, picking up pieces of wrapping paper and putting them in a large garbage bag. She has on a green sweater, tan pants, and her socks have Christmas trees on them, and she's dancing to Christmas music playing from the antique record player in the corner of the room. 'It's the best time of the year.'

'You say that about Halloween and Thanksgiving, too,' I say, glancing at Kayden, who has a fist balled in front of his mouth to hide his chuckling at my mother's madness. It's so embarrassing, but I'm trying my hardest not to get embarrassed because I need to get used to it – Kayden learning all my family's little quirks.

'And Valentine's Day and the Fourth of July,' my

dad says as he stacks the presents we just opened in a corner. He has on a red and green sweatshirt my mother made him wear all day to celebrate the festivities. 'Not to mention New Year's.'

'Oh, I have so many plans for New Year's.' My mother sets the bag down and walks over to me, beaming. 'I was thinking you and I could go shopping, get our hair done, then we could all go out to dinner.' She glances at Kayden before looking at me. 'All four of us.'

I open my mouth to say . . . well, something that will get us out of that mess, but my father chimes in, giving me a devious look. 'Actually, sweetie, I had something really special planned for you and me.'

'Really?' My mother claps her hands together and rushes over to him to give him a big hug.

Run, my dad mouths from over my mother's shoulder with a grin. *Run while you can.*

He doesn't have to ask me twice. I snatch ahold of Kayden's hand and yank him out of the living room.

'Oh my God,' I hiss, guiding Kayden by the sleeve of his shirt across the kitchen and toward the back door away from my mother. Once we're out of the house, I pick up the pace, hurrying across the driveway to the garage, worried my mother's going to follow us.

'I seriously think she's like one step away from locking us in the house so she can keep us forever.'

Kayden chuckles, amused by my embarrassment as he pinches my cheeks, like my mom has done to me a thousand times. 'What can I say? I'm super lovable enough to want to keep me forever.' He's quoting something my mother said to him earlier when we were opening presents.

'You are lovable,' I tell him once we get inside the guest room above the garage and the door is safely shut behind us. And locked. 'But she doesn't need to tell you that every minute.' I flop down on my back onto the air mattress, which is the only piece of furniture besides the space heater and the bathroom. I'm not complaining, though, since the reason it's so bare is because the furniture now fills our apartment.

'She's just being nice,' Kayden says, gazing down at me. His hair is ruffled, his jawline is scruffy, and he looks so happy. 'And it's nice that she wants to be so nice. It could be worse than an overnice mother.'

'Yeah, I know,' I sigh, knowing he's right, that it could be worse, that I could have parents like his mother. 'I just wish she'd be just a little bit less embarrassing.' I raise my hand and make a pinching gesture with my fingers. 'Maybe just a teeny, tiny bit.'

'Yeah, I doubt that's ever going to happen.' Kayden slips his shirt off and chucks it aside. His jeans ride low on his hips, giving me a view of his abs and chest that is crisscrossed with scars. 'I did find it funny when she kept cracking jokes about us getting married all through dinner.' He kneels down on the mattress, nudging my knees open with his until I spread open my legs for him.

'Oh God.' Shaking my head, I cover my face with my hands. 'I'm glad you find it funny because I'm sure most guys would be running for their lives.'

The mattress moves as he leans over me and puts a hand on each side of my head. I crack my fingers apart and look at him. He's been so much happier since the funeral, since he said goodbye to his mother, since he put the past behind him. He seems to breathe freer, smile more, and it's probably the most beautiful sight I've ever seen.

'Well, just make sure you really want this,' I say as he moves one of my hands away from my eyes, 'because you still have time to run.'

He shakes his head, his tongue slipping out of his mouth to wet his lips. 'No running here,' he whispers in a raspy voice I know only means one thing – he wants me. 'Ever.' He moves my other hand away from my face then pins my arms above my head.

A while ago, the movement would have sent my heart soaring and not in a good way. But now . . . well, it freaking soars like a bird high up in the sky, never wanting to return to land, ever. It soars because it's free. It soars for him.

'You want me,' I tease as he leans down to kiss me.

'You're right,' he says. 'And then I want to give you your present.'

'But you already gave me my present.' I pat my pocket, inside which are the tickets to the concert he gave me. He said it was for a redo of a night that should have been special, but he couldn't give it to me then. He was ready now to give me everything I deserve – his words not mine. My mom practically fainted when he said it. And me . . . well, I think I fell in love with Kayden even more.

'Yeah, but that one was only the first part.' He kisses me then softly bites my bottom lip before he leans back for air. 'There's more,' he breathes against my lips, coming in for another kiss, 'but you have to wait.'

'Until when?' I wonder, my heart skipping a beat as his hands wander to the button of my jeans.

'Until we're done with this.' He gives me a wicked smile as he flicks my button undone.

'That feels like blackmail . . .' My back arches as his knuckles graze my stomach. 'Good thing I like being blackmailed by you.'

'God, I love that look in your eyes when I touch you,' he says softly against my ear before nipping at my lobe.

I'm about to get lost inside him when I remember something. 'Wait.' I put a hand against his chest, pushing him back a little, causing him to give a sexy, frustrated growl that makes the area between my lips tingle. 'Don't you want your present?'

He pushes back from me and arches his brow. 'What? I thought that sweater was from all of you.' He's totally amused with himself.

I glare at him. 'You did not. I would never, ever be a part of giving you a sweater with an elf knitted on it.'

'Hey, I like the sweater,' he insists, actually being genuine. 'No one has ever given me a sweater. Fuck, no one has ever given me a present before.'

Wow, I can feel the pressure. Maybe I should have gotten something better than I did.

'Well, don't get too excited,' I say, scooting out from under him and rolling off the mattress. 'It's not much.' I reach into my duffel bag to get his present.

He sits up on the mattress, looking about as eager as a kid sitting in front of a Christmas tree. 'I'll be happy with whatever you give me.'

I know he's telling the truth, but still, when I hand him the small, rectangular present, I feel like it's not enough. I hold my breath in anticipation and sit down beside him as he tears the paper off and chucks it aside. I wait for his reaction, but he just sits there, frozen, staring at it.

He stares.

And stares.

And stares.

With his head is tucked down and I can't read him at all.

'I told you I took pictures of us.' I tap the frame that's around the picture of Kayden and me kissing at the carnival we went to this summer. It's actually a really pretty picture, the flashing neon lights and shapes of the rides behind us contrasting perfectly with the starry night above us. 'Well, Seth actually took this one with my phone, but it's a gorgeous photo of us. Totally wall-worthy, I think.'

He just keeps staring at the photo and I feel like I'm about to lose my mind as I think of all the things that could be wrong. Maybe I'm reminding him of his past too much. Maybe I'm reminding him of everything he didn't have.

But when I finally work up the courage to say something, a tear slips from his eye.

He's crying and I'm afraid.

Maybe this was too emotional.

Maybe it was the wrong thing.

As my self-doubts wash over me, he lifts his gaze to meet mine and I realize that I was wrong.

He's not crying because he's sad.

He's crying because he feels loved.

And good God do I love him. More than anything else in the world.

He doesn't say anything. He just attacks me, his lips crashing into mine and stealing the breath right out of my lungs. But that's okay; I'll give him my air, my heart, my soul, whatever he wants. The only thing that matters is that he wants it.

'You remember the last time we were in this room?' he says through his panting as we finally come up for air.

I nod, gazing up at his swollen lips before allowing my eyes to rest on his. 'I do.' It was the first time we made love.

'It was one of the most amazing moments of my

life,' he says softly, his body heat warming every inch of me. 'Did you know that?' he asks. When I shake my head, he whispers, 'Well, it was. And even though I didn't know it at the time, it was the moment I fell in love with you.'

His words sink through my skin and shoot straight to my heart. 'I think it was when I fell in love with you, too,' I whisper.

There's a pause. A silent exchange that words can't express.

Then we start ripping off each other's clothes. Buttons fly. Fabric gets thrown. We're laughing and smiling and he's crying and so am I for reasons I can't even understand. It's like I'm feeling everything all at once and it's so overwhelming and powerful, and I wouldn't trade it for anything in the world. And when he slips inside me, his body over mine, all I can think of is how safe I feel in a place that once felt like it was surrounded by thorns and vines. A place that felt so unsafe. A place where I lost it all, but now I'm being given it all back and more.

And no, Kayden is not my prince. Nor have I become a princess again.

I am simply Callie.

And he is simply Kayden.

And we are simply us.

And it's the realest form of perfection that's ever existed.

'What are you doing?' Kayden asks as I sit up from the mattress and stretch my hands over my head. It's late, well past midnight, and I've been lying there for what feels like hours, trying to fall asleep, but it wasn't working for me. My brain is on. And I mean, on. With words and sentences begging to be written.

'Nothing.' I reach for his shirt and slip it over my head. 'I was just going to do a little writing because I can't sleep.'

He rolls to his side and props up on his elbow as I move for my bag to get my laptop. 'So when do I get to read this mystery story?' he asks, tracing his fingers up and down my spine.

I consider what he said as I run back on the mattress, hurrying because the carpetless floor is freezing my feet. 'When it's finished.'

He glances from the laptop to me then cocks his brow. 'And when will that be?'

I lean against the wall and position the laptop on my lap. 'Probably tonight. I can feel the ending getting nearer.' I open the computer and click on the screen. 'Or at least the open-ending one.'

'What's it about?' He leans over and reads the title on the screen. 'The Truthful Fairytale.' His gaze travels up to me. 'It sounds like it's about a princess and a prince.'

I shake my head as I put a pillow behind my back and stretch out my legs. 'Nope. Just a boy and a girl.'

He gives me a curious look. 'But you'll let me read it, right? I love reading your stuff. I swear it gives me a little insight into what goes on in that head of yours.'

'Which is sure madness.' I do my best evil villain voice and he laughs. 'And yes, I promise you'll get to read it when it's done.'

Seeming satisfied, he lies back down and gets comfortable. I only start really writing, though, when he falls asleep; otherwise, I feel like he's watching me.

The first date was magical. They ate. They danced. They laughed. They smiled. By the end of the night, the air was so electric the girl had to glance around because it seriously felt like there were fairies hiding in the bushes, sprinkling pixie dust wherever they went.

'I'm glad we did this,' the guy said as they walked up a path they'd never taken before, side by side.

'I'm glad, too,' she replied. 'I had a lot of fun.' And it

was the truth. *She did have fun and it almost made the night surreal. Maybe she was dreaming. Maybe she'd fallen asleep and none of this was real. If that was the case, then she hoped she'd never wake up.*

The stars and the moon shone above them and the houses around them were fast asleep. It was just them. No monsters. No expectations. No kingdoms and queens and kings and palaces.

It was perfect.

And for the first time in a long time, the girl felt safe.

Maybe even daring.

With every ounce of bravery she could summon, she reached over and took the boy's hand in hers. She half expected him to recoil from the contact, half expected to do the same thing herself. Instead, the boy held on and she gripped tighter.

There wasn't a spark or a zap from the contact, just a rush of energy as their flesh touched for the first time.

'You know, I never would have been here if it wasn't for you,' he said so abruptly it threw her off guard.

'What do you mean?' she asked, stopping with the boy beneath a lamppost. It was the only light on the street and it surrounded them.

He looked down at her with such passion in his eyes, begging for her to understand. 'That night when you came . . . *when you saved me, it changed the direction of my life.'*

The girl felt breathless. 'How so?'

'Because I'd given up,' he said, daring to graze his finger down her cheek, causing her to shudder and her heart to skip a beat. *'I thought the world was full of monsters and there wasn't really a point in fighting them anymore. That wherever I'd go, they'd be there to break me, but you . . . you showed me not everyone was a monster.'*

'You showed me that, too,' the girl replied. *The boy looked at her, confused, and she wanted to explain, but she couldn't just yet.*

Maybe that was the key to all this, after all? Not the key to getting her back to being a princess. She didn't want to be a princess anymore, knew better than to believe in such things. But what she did want to be was a normal girl who could hold hands with a guy without feeling ugly and disgusted.

She just wanted to be happy in her own little world.

'I wish I could do more,' he replied with a sad expression.

She didn't want him to be sad, though.

She wanted him to be happy.

The both of them.

But she had to wonder if maybe he could do more. Or maybe she had to do it herself. Maybe she was the one who had to be brave, to save herself.

Without even thinking, she started to lean in to kiss him, hoping she wouldn't scare him. To her surprise, he leaned in, too, and the two of them met in the middle.

The joining of their lips didn't set off an explosion of fireworks. There was no music announcing this was the starting point of their happily ever after. In fact, the light above them flickered off and there was nothing but darkness. But it couldn't smother the light caused by the fire hidden deep inside each other's hearts, a fire that could quite possibly burn forever if they chose to let it.

And it was a start.

To happiness.

To a life without monsters controlling them.

And really, that's all both of them ever wanted.

Not a happily ever after.

Just a happy after.

I'm not sure how long I stare at the screen, deciding if that's it, but I'm pretty sure it's at least it for an hour. After the hour's up, though, I decide I'm happy with it and save it in my portfolio file. Then I lean over to put my computer aside on the floor, not wanting to get out of bed and out from beneath the covers. The room is dark, the only light coming through the window of the door where I can see the moon up in the sky.

'I forgot to give you your present,' Kayden says so abruptly I let out a blood-curdling scream.

'Oh my God, you scared me.' I catch my breath through his hysterical laughing. 'I thought you were asleep.'

'No, I've been awake.' He stifles his laughter and sits up, reaching for his duffel bag that's beside the bed.

'This entire time?'

He unzips the bag. 'Yeah, I was watching you write.'

'That sounds super boring.' I lie down in the bed and turn on my side to face him.

'Actually, it was super entertaining.' He grabs something from his bag, flips on a lamp nearby, and then turns to me. There's a small, silver box in his hand and a sparkle in his eyes. 'Merry Christmas.' He gives me the box as he lies back down beside me.

I wait a moment or two, trying not to think too hard about what's in it. Finally, I just open it.

Then I stop breathing.

'Oh my God, you didn't have to do this . . .' I whisper in awe.

'I know I didn't,' Kayden says, watching me with a smile on his face, 'but I wanted to.'

Inside the box is probably one of the coolest necklaces I've seen. It's in no way traditional, which makes me love it even more. The silver pendant is shaped like a book, and when I pick it up, I noticed it's engraved on the front with *By Callie Lawrence*. It also opens up like a locket but the inside is blank, like fresh pages ready to be stained with a story.

'Do you like it?' he finally asks and I realize that beneath his grin, he's waiting for my approval.

'It's perfect,' I say then lean over to kiss him.

'Good,' he says between kisses. 'I'm glad you like it. It's for when you write your story. To show I believe in you.'

I almost start crying right there. 'I love it.' I put the necklace on, promising to never take it off. Then I lie down and snuggle against him beneath the covers, feeling more content than I ever have.

I'm about to fall asleep when he asks, 'Can I read it now?'

My eyelids lift open. 'Read what?'

'Your story,' he says with a lopsided grin as he stares down at me expectantly. 'I saw you type "The End."'

I suddenly get nervous and my palms get so sweaty I have to wipe them off on the front of my shirt. 'You want to read it right now?'

He nods enthusiastically. 'I do.'

'Um . . . okay.' I turn over and reach for my laptop, feeling even more anxious. I hope he likes it, hope he understands it, because really, he's half the story.

And one of the most important parts.

He tells me I can go to sleep while he reads it, but there's no way I can shut my eyes. So I end up lying there, staring at all the patches in the ceiling until he finishes. I know the exact moment he does because I can hear his breathing quicken. Then he sets the laptop aside and rolls over to me. He just stares at me and I can't read him at all.

'So what'd you think?' I ask, aiming for indifferent but ending up sounding like a bundle of nerves.

He's silent for forever, each second passing almost painfully slow. 'I think it's beautiful and meaningful and real,' he finally says, his tone radiating every emotion he's feeling. 'Although, I'm pretty sure ours gets a happily ever after.'

'You think so?' I ask with a soft smile. 'Because that's a big promise.'

His smile reflects mine. 'No, I know so.'

And then he kisses me.

But this isn't the end of our story just yet.

In fact, it kind of feels like the beginning.

Chapter 27

#103 ~~Outrun~~ Leave Your Inner Demons Behind and Find Your Love for the Game.

Kayden

It's the last game of the season and I'm feeling pretty good. Things have been amazing with Callie and I've been focusing on the future instead of the past. It's been that way for the last month, ever since I said my goodbye. I'm not happy all the time, though, but then again no one ever is. I still feel the slightest bit of guilt and sadness whenever I think of my father and how it all ended, but that happens very rarely.

What almost always happens is that I'm happy, not just with my relationship with Callie, but with myself. It took me forever to get to this place, to let go, but I've managed to find my own form of inner peace with all that happened to me. And I can honestly say that my life is great at the moment.

Right now, I'm fucking amped up, though, as I get ready to make the last play of the game. If we don't make it, we lose, but I'm not betting on us losing, In fact, I can feel it in the air, in the hollers of the crowd, in the lights that are so fucking bright it's blinding. From the fucking way that I'm loving every minute of this.

My team is lined up and I'm hunched over, waiting for the snap. My heart is thudding, my skin damp with sweat, my feet ready. And my mind . . .

Is silent.

I hear everything. From the sound of the footsteps, to my coach shouting something on the sidelines. I can also hear my own voice.

You can do it.

I know I can.

My heart slams against my chest as the ball is snapped in my directions. My fingers perfectly wrap around it and then I'm running back, looking for the perfect throw. But then I realize there's no perfect through, but a close one. So I spring my arm back and let the ball slip from my fingers and soar away.

I let it all soar away as I breathe freely for the first time, waiting for it to happen.

The ball climbs higher and so does my pulse. I swear the crowd is holding their breaths, but maybe that's because I'm holding mine as I watch the ball reach its peak and then drop.

It drops.

And drops.

And drops.

Then it lands perfectly in the receiver's hands.

Perfect.

Touchdown!

The crowd starts cheering and so do my teammates as we win the game. And this time I join them, cheering and happy as I look up at the crowd where I know Callie is watching me with pride. But only part of my celebration is because I kicked ass and played my heart out. The other part is because I've finally left my inner demons behind and found my love for the game.

Epilogue

A little over a year later . . .

#595 Make Your Happy After Official (Because It's About Damn Time)

Callie

Life is great. Not perfect, but life never is. But perfection would be boring anyway. For the most part, things are good, though. Kayden and I are still living together, and plan to stay that way for a while. Our walls are covered in photos of us as a couple, with family, with friends. It shows how whole our lives are and how far we've both come.

There's been a lot of talk about him getting drafted next year, though, and we did have the talk even though it's early. It only took us like two minutes of him laying out all the reasons why he needs me to come with him if he leaves Laramie, and it took me like half a second to sputter that I'd follow him anywhere, that I can write anywhere, since that's what I've been doing and plan to keep doing. That a life without him would be a sad life I never want to have.

We have a little routine now where we alternate holidays between my parents' house and his brother's in Virginia. I got to meet a sober Tyler about six months ago and that was nice. And Kayden hasn't cut himself in just over a year. The sadness in his eyes is gone, except for on occasion, like when he gets a random call from his mother. He never answers her, though, or calls her back, and her voicemails are anything but persuading.

But other than the occasional sadness and silly fights, Kayden and I are going strong. He tells me every day that he loves me and I tell him every day how important he is to me. Our happy after is working quite well for us and seems to only get better in time. It makes me excited for what the future holds – our future. Makes me excited that we have a future.

'Writing again, I see.' Seth interrupts my thoughts as he strolls into my living room without even knocking.

He doesn't bother to shut the door either, even though it's freezing outside and a light gust of snow blows in.

'What if I hadn't been dressed?' I joke, closing my journal. It's filled with so many pages of my pen that ink is seriously starting to stain the edges.

He rolls his eyes. 'Yeah, right. You would never be naked in your living room.' He pauses then gets this scandalous look on his face. 'I, on the other hand, make it a daily ritual.'

Now I'm the one rolling my eyes. 'Oh, whatever.' I toss the journal on the coffee table as I get to my feet. 'So are you going to shut the door or are you trying to add to my heating bill?' I grin at him.

He shakes his head, but is amused. 'Actually, it's time to go to the game.'

My forehead creases as I glance at the time on my phone. 'But it's super early.' Like hours early.

'I know,' he says, picking up my coat from the armrest and tossing it to me, 'but I was instructed to take you there early.'

'By who?' I ask as I slip my arms through the sleeves of my coat and zip it up.

'It's a secret.' Then he winks at me and heads out the door, leaving me utterly confused.

I follow him outside, locking the door before I trot

down the stairs behind him. There's a light frost on the ground and the air is nipping, but the sun is shining and the reflection of it against the snow makes everything sparkle. I can't help but breathe in the magicalness of the air before getting into the car.

Seth's grinning by the time I shut the door as he starts up the engine and then backs out.

'You're acting weird,' I tell him as I buckle my seatbelt. 'What's up?'

He shrugs as he turns the steering wheel and we head toward the street. 'Nothing.'

I know Seth enough to know that he's lying. 'You're so full of it. What's going on . . .? Why are you taking me early?'

'It's a surprise,' he says, pulling out onto the street.

'Please, pretty please, tell me,' I beg with my hands clasped in front of me.

He shakes his head. 'No way. Not this time.'

'I won't tell anyone.'

'It doesn't matter, Callie. I'd be mad at myself if I ruined this one for you.'

I pout as I slump back in the seat. 'Oh, fine. I'll play along.' I fiddle with the stereo until I find a good song, then I try to relax, but as we pass by a bookstore something dawns on me.

'Oh, crap.' I put a hand to the base of my neck. 'I forgot my necklace.' It's the one Kayden gave me for Christmas that has a book pendant with my name on it.

'You'll be fine for one game, Callie,' Seth brushes me off.

'No way. We have to go back. It brings him good luck whenever I wear it.'

Seth chuckles as he turns off the main road toward the shiny, steel stadium. 'You two and your superstition.'

'It's not a superstition,' I say, which isn't quite the truth, but Kayden says that whenever I wear it, it brings him good luck when he plays. Growing up with a father for a football coach, I know enough to tolerate these superstitions.

'Relax, Callie,' Seth tells me as he parks the car near the entrance of the stadium. 'I have your necklace.'

'Why do you have it?' I wonder.

There's a pause and I feel the shift in the air. Something's happening. Something important.

Seth looks like he's about to cry as he reaches over, takes my hand, turns it palm up, and drops the necklace into it. 'Don't look at it until you get into the stadium.' He closes my fingers around it then sits back in his seat. 'Now go.'

I glance down at my hand and then to the stadium,

knowing without really knowing that something magical is about to happen. Unable to form words, I get out of the car and make my journey toward the stadium with the necklace clutched in my hand. The security asks my name then lets me through when I tell him.

I walk down the tunnel and onto the field, smiling when I remember the night Kayden took me here over two years ago to play catch. And to make out pressed up against the field post. It seems smaller this time, though, less overwhelming. Honestly, I feel like I kind of belong here.

The feeling only amplifies when Kayden emerges from behind me. I take in his brown hair hanging in his gorgeous eyes I swear can read my soul now. And his lean arms and broad shoulders that hold me whenever I feel sad. He's dressed not in his uniform but in jeans, boots, and his coat, which I find a little odd.

'Hey, you made it,' he says as he casually walks toward me, like this isn't at all weird.

'Yeah, but I'm wondering why I needed to make it,' I say with suspicion, tipping my head back to look up at him as he reaches me. 'I'm guessing you and Seth have something major planned, though, since the two of you never plot together unless it's something epic.'

'Oh, it's definitely epic,' he says in a cocky tone,

but his eyes reveal otherwise. He's nervous and that makes me nervous.

'Okay . . .?' My fingers tighten around the necklace. 'Would you like to share with me what this epicness is?'

He nods, but swallows hard, his skin suddenly paling. 'A-actually,' he starts to stammer, but then clears his throat and shakes his head at himself. 'Okay, let me try *that* again.' We both laugh, but not because this is funny – because we're nervous.

'Do you remember the last time you and I were out here?' he asks, motioning at the field and the bleachers enclosing it.

I nod. 'Yeah, I kicked your ass at catch.'

He laughs, his eyes bright, but his nerves still there. 'You did, didn't you?' He pauses, tugging his fingers through his hair. 'Well, I thought I'd bring you back here so we could relive another good past memory since we haven't done this one before.'

Is that what this is about? 'You want to play catch again?'

He shakes his head. 'No, I want to ask you something.'

'Okay . . .?' I'm so confused.

And he's looking paler by the second.

'Do you have your necklace?' he asks, his voice almost as soft as a whisper.

I nod then open my hand. 'Yeah, Seth told me not to look at it until I got to the stadium.' There's a pause and then he nervously waits for me to catch on. 'Oh, right.' I laugh at myself as I look down at the book pendant in my hand.

And then I see it.

What all of this is about?

'By Callie Lawrence-Owens,' I read aloud, sounding more nervous than him.

'Open it.' This time, he does whisper.

With trembling fingers, I fumble with the clasp and finally get it open. The pages are no longer blank. They are filled with the promise of a story. And it's the most amazing story ever.

Your happily ever after.

'Yes!' I cry before he can even ask. Then I throw my arms around his neck and hug him with everything I have in me.

He laughs at me and whispers a, 'Thank God,' sounding extremely happy as he returns my hug equally, giving me the best thing in the world.

Not just my happy after.

But him.

Have you read the first book in
the story of Callie and Kayden?
Find out how it all began in
The Coincidence of Callie & Kayden . . .

Read an extract here –
the book is available to buy now.

Prologue

Callie

Life is full of luck, like getting dealt a good hand, or simply by being in the right place at the right time. Some people get luck handed to them, a second chance, a save. It can happen heroically, or by a simple co-incidence, but there are those who don't get luck on a shiny platter, who end up in the wrong place at the wrong time, who don't get saved.

'Callie, are you listening to me?' my mom asks as she parks the car in the driveway.

I don't answer, watching the leaves twirl in the wind across the yard, the hood of the car, wherever the breeze forces them to go. They have no control over their path in life. I have a desire to jump out, grab them all, and clutch them in my hand, but that would mean getting out of the car.

'What is wrong with you tonight?' my mom snaps as she checks her phone messages. 'Just go in and get your brother.'

I tear my gaze off the leaves and focus on her. 'Please don't make me do this, Mom.' My sweaty hand grips the metal door handle and a massive lump lodges in my throat. 'Can't you just go in and get him?'

'I have no desire to go into a party with a bunch of high-school kids and I'm really not in the mood to chat it up with Maci right now, so she can brag about Kayden getting a scholarship,' my mother replies, motioning her manicured hand at me to get a move on. 'Now go get your brother and tell him he needs to come home.'

My shoulders hunch as I push the door open and hike up the gravel driveway toward the two-story mansion with green shutters and a steep roof. 'Two more days, two more days,' I chant under my breath with my hands clenched into fists as I squeeze between the vehicles. 'Only two more days and I'll be in college and none of this will matter.'

The lights through the windows illuminate against the gray sky and a 'Congratulations' banner hangs above the entrance to the porch, decorated with balloons. The Owenses always like to put on a show, for any reason they can think of: birthdays, holidays, graduations. They seem like the perfect family but I don't believe in perfection.

This party is to celebrate their youngest son Kayden's graduation and his football scholarship to the University of Wyoming. I have nothing against the Owenses. My family has dinner over at their house occasionally and they attend barbecues at our place. I just don't like parties, nor have I been welcomed at one, at least since sixth grade.

When I approach the wraparound porch, Daisy McMillian waltzes out with a glass in her hand. Her curly blonde hair shines in the porch light as her eyes aim at me and a malicious grin curls at her lips.

I dodge to the right of the stairs and swerve around the side of the house before she can insult me. The sun is lowering below the lines of the mountains that encase the town and stars sparkle across the sky like dragonflies. It's hard to see once the lights of the front porch fade away, and my shoe catches something sharp. I fall down and my palms split open against the gravel. Injuries on the outside are easy to endure and I get up without hesitation.

I dust the pebbles from my hands, wincing from the burn of the scratches as I round the corner into the backyard.

'I don't give a shit what the hell you were trying to do,' a male voice cuts through the darkness. 'You're such a fuckup. A fucking disappointment.'

I halt by the edge of the grass. Near the back fence is a brick pool house where two figures stand below a dim light. One is taller, with his head hanging low and his broad shoulders stooped. The shorter one has a beer gut, a bald spot on the back of his head, and is standing in the other's face with his fists out in front of him. Squinting through the dark, I make out that the shorter one is Mr. Owens and the taller one is Kayden Owens. The situation is surprising since Kayden is very confident at school and has never been much of a target for violence.

'I'm sorry,' Kayden mutters with a tremor in his voice as he hugs his hand against his chest. 'It was an accident, sir. I won't do it again.'

I glance at the open back door where the lights are on, the music is loud, and people are dancing, shouting, laughing. Glasses clink together and I can feel the sexual tension bottled in the room from all the way out here. These are the kinds of places I avoid at all cost, because I can't breathe very well in them. I move up to the bottom step tentatively, hoping to disappear into the crowd unnoticed, find my brother, and get the hell out of here.

'Don't fucking tell me it was an accident!' The voice rises, blazing with incomprehensible rage. There's a loud bang and then a crack, like bones splitting into pieces. Instinctively I whirl around just in time to see Mr. Owens smash his fist into Kayden's face. The crack makes my gut churn. He hits him again and again, not stopping even when Kayden crumples to the ground. 'Liars get punished, Kayden.'

I wait for Kayden to get back up, but he stays unmoving, not even bothering to cover his face with his arms. His father kicks him in the stomach, in the face, his movements harder, showing no sign of an approaching end.

I react without thinking, a desire to save him burning so fiercely it washes all doubts from my mind. I run across the grass and through the leaves blowing in the air without a plan other than to interrupt. When I reach them, I'm shaking and verging toward shock as it becomes clear the situation is larger than my mind originally grasped.

Mr. Owens's knuckles are gashed and blood drips

onto the cement in front of the pool house. Kayden is on the ground, his cheekbone cut open like a crack in the bark of a tree. His eye is swollen shut, his lip is ruptured, and there is blood all over his face.

Their eyes move to me and I quickly point over my shoulder with a very unsteady finger. 'There was someone looking for you in the kitchen,' I say to Mr. Owens, thankful that for once my voice maintains steadiness. 'They needed help with something... I can't remember what, though.'

His sharp gaze pierces into me and I cower back at the anger and powerlessness in his eyes, like his rage controls him. 'Who the hell are you?'

'Callie Lawrence,' I say quietly, noting the smell of liquor on his breath.

His gaze travels from my worn shoes to the heavy black jacket with buckles, and finally lands on my hair that barely brushes my chin. I look like a homeless person, but that's the point. I want to be unnoticed. 'Oh, yeah, you're Coach Lawrence's daughter. I didn't recognize you in the dark.' He glances down at the blood on his knuckles and then looks back at me. 'Listen, Callie, I didn't mean for this to happen. It was an accident.'

I don't do well under pressure so I stand motionless, listening to my heart knock inside my chest. 'Okay.'

'I need to go clean up,' he mutters. His gaze bores into me for a brief moment before he stomps across the grass toward the back door with his injured hand clasped beside him.

I focus back on Kayden, releasing a breath trapped in my chest. 'Are you okay?'

He cups his hand over his eye, stares at his shoes, and keeps his other hand against his chest, seeming vulnerable, weak, and perplexed. For a second, I picture myself on the ground with bruises and cuts that can only be seen from the inside.

'I'm fine.' His voice is harsh, so I turn toward the house, ready to bolt.

'Why did you do that?' he calls out through the darkness.

I stop on the line of the grass and turn to meet his eyes. 'I did what anyone else would have done.'

The eyebrow above his good eye dips down. 'No, you didn't.'

Kayden and I have gone to school together since we were in kindergarten. Sadly this is the longest conversation we've had since about sixth grade, when I was deemed the class weirdo. In the middle of the year, I showed up to school with my hair chopped off and wearing clothes that nearly swallowed me. After that,

I lost all my friends. Even when our families have dinner together, Kayden pretends like he doesn't know me.

'You did what almost no one would have done.' Lowering his hand from his eye, he staggers to his feet and towers over me as he straightens his legs. He is the kind of guy girls have an infatuation for, including me back when I saw guys as something else other than a threat. His brown hair flips at his ears and neck, his usually perfect smile is a bloody mess, and only one of his emerald eyes is visible. 'I don't understand why you did it.'

I scratch at my forehead, my nervous habit when someone is really seeing me. 'Well, I couldn't just walk away. I'd never be able to forgive myself if I did.'

The light from the house emphasizes the severity of his wounds and there is blood splattered all over his shirt. 'You can't tell anyone about this, okay? He's been drinking…and going through some stuff. He's not himself tonight.'

I bite at my lip, unsure if I believe him. 'Maybe you should tell someone…like your mom.'

He stares at me like I'm a small, incompetent child. 'There's nothing to tell.'

I eye his puffy face, his normally perfect features now distorted. 'All right, if that's what you want.'

'It's what I want,' he says dismissively and I start to walk away. 'Hey Callie, it's Callie, right? Will you do me a favor?'

I peer over my shoulder. 'Sure. What?'

'In the downstairs bathroom there's a first-aid kit, and in the freezer there's an icepack. Would you go grab them for me? I don't want to go in until I've cleaned up.'

I'm desperate to leave, but the pleading in his tone overpowers me. 'Yes, I can do that.' I leave him near the pool house to go inside, and the very crowded atmosphere makes it hard to breathe. Tucking in my elbows and hoping no one will touch me, I weave through the people.

Maci Owens, Kayden's mother, is chatting with some of the other moms at the table and waves her hand at me, her gold and silver bangle bracelets jingling together. 'Oh Callie, is your mom here, hun?' Her speech is slurred and there is an empty bottle of wine in front of her.

'She's out in the car,' I call out over the music as someone bumps into my shoulder and my muscles stiffen. 'She was on the phone with my dad and sent me in to find my brother. Have you seen him?'

'Sorry, hun, I haven't.' She motions her hand around with flourish. 'There are just so many people here.'

I give her a small wave. 'Okay, well, I'm going to go look for him.' As I walk away, I wonder if she's seen her husband and if she'll question the cut on his hand.

In the living room, my brother Jackson is sitting on the sofa, talking to his best friend, Caleb Miller. I freeze near the threshold, just out of their sight. They keep laughing and talking, drinking their beers, like nothing matters. I despise my brother for laughing, for being here, for making it so I have to go tell him Mom is waiting out in the car.

I start toward him, but I can't get my feet to move. I know I need to get it over with, but there are people making out in the corners and dancing in the middle of the room and it's making me uncomfortable. *I can't breathe. I can't breathe. Move feet, move.*

Someone runs into me and it nearly knocks me to the floor.

'Sorry,' a deep voice apologizes.

I catch myself on the doorframe and it breaks my trance. I hurry down the hall without bothering to see who ran into me. I need to get out of this place and breathe again.

After I collect the first-aid kit from the bottom cupboard and the icepack from the freezer, I take the long way out of the house, going through the side door unnoticed. Kayden's not outside anymore, but the interior light of the pool house filters from the windows.

Hesitantly, I push open the door and poke my head into the dimly lit room. 'Hello.'

Kayden walks out from the back room without a shirt on and a towel pressed up to his face, which is bright red and lumpy. 'Hey, did you get the stuff?'

I slip into the room and shut the door behind me. I hold out the first-aid kit and the icepack, with my head turned toward the door to avoid looking at him. His bare chest, and the way his jeans ride low on his hips smothers me with uneasiness.

'I don't bite, Callie.' His tone is neutral as he takes the kit and the pack. 'You don't have to stare at the wall.'

I compel my eyes to look at him and it's hard not to stare at the scars that crisscross along his stomach and chest. The vertical lines that run down his forearms are the most disturbing, thick and jagged as if someone took a razor to his skin. I wish I could run my fingers along them and remove the pain and memories that are attached to them.

He quickly lowers the towel to cover himself up and

confusion gleams from his good eye as we stare at one another. My heart throbs inside my chest as a moment passes, like a snap of a finger, yet it seems to go on forever.

He blinks and presses the pack to his inflamed eye while balancing the kit on the edge of the pool table. His fingers quiver as he pulls his hand back and each knuckle is scraped raw. 'Can you get the gauze out of that for me? My hand's a little sore.'

As my fingers fumble to lift the latch, my fingernail catches in the crack, and it peels back. Blood pools out as I open the lid to retrieve the gauze. 'You might need stitches on that cut below the eye. It looks bad.'

He dabs the cut with the towel, wincing from the pain. 'It'll be fine. I just need to clean it up and get it covered.'

The steaming hot water runs down my body, scorching my skin with red marks and blisters. I just want to feel clean again. I take the damp towel from him, careful not to let our fingers touch, and lean forward to examine the lesion, which is so deep the muscle and tissue is showing.

'You really need stitches.' I suck the blood off my thumb. 'Or you're going to have a scar.'

The corners of his lips tug up into a sad smile. 'I can handle scars, especially ones that are on the outside.'

I understand his meaning from the depths of my heart. 'I really think you should have your mom take you to the doctor and then you can tell her what happened.'

He starts to unwind a small section of gauze, but he accidentally drops it onto the floor. 'That'll never happen and even if it did, it wouldn't matter. None of this does.'

With unsteady fingers, I gather up the gauze and unravel it around my hand. Tearing the end, I grab the tape out of the kit. Then squeezing every last terrified thought from my mind, I reach toward his cheek. He remains very still, hugging his sore hand against his chest as I place the gauze over the wound. His eyes stay on me, his brows knit, and he barely breathes as I tape it in place.

I pull back and an exhale eases out of my lips. He's the first person I've intentionally touched outside my family for the last six years. 'I would still consider getting stitches.'

He closes the kit and wipes a droplet of blood off the lid. 'Did you see my father inside?'

'No.' My phone beeps from my pocket and I read

over the text message. 'I have to go. My mom's waiting
out in the car. Are you sure you'll be okay?'

'I'll be fine.' He doesn't glance up at me as he picks
up the towel and heads toward the back room. 'All
right, I'll see you later, I guess.'

No, you won't. Putting my phone away in my pocket,
I depart for the door. 'Yeah, I guess I'll see you later.'

'Thank you,' he instantly adds.

I pause with my hand on the doorknob. I feel terrible
for leaving him, but I'm too chicken to stay behind.
'For what?'

He deliberates for an eternity and then exhales a
sigh. 'For getting me the first-aid kit and icepack.'

'You're welcome.' I walk out the door with a heavy
feeling in my heart as another secret falls on top of it.

As the gravel driveway comes into view, my phone
rings from inside my pocket. 'I'm like two feet away,'
I answer.

'Your brother is out here and he needs to get home.
He's got to be at the airport in eight hours.' My mother's
tone is anxious.

I increase my pace. 'Sorry, I got sidetracked...but
you sent me in to get him.'

'Well, he answered his text, now come on,' she says
frantically. 'He needs to get some rest.'

'I'll be there in like thirty seconds, Mom.' I hang up as I step out into the front yard.

Daisy, Kayden's girlfriend, is out on the front porch, eating a slice of cake as she chats with Caleb Miller. My insides instantly knot, my shoulders slouch, and I shy into the shadows of the trees, hoping they won't see me.

'Oh my God, is that Callie Lawrence?' Daisy says, shielding her eyes with her hand and squinting in my direction. 'What the heck are you doing here? Shouldn't you be like hanging out at the cemetery or something?'

I tuck my chin down and pick up the pace, stumbling over a large rock. *One foot in front of the other.*

'Or are you just running away from the piece of cake I have?' she yells with laughter in her tone. 'Which one is it Callie? Come on, tell me?'

'Knock it off,' Caleb warns with a smirk on his face as he leans over the railing, his eyes as black as the night. 'I'm sure Callie has her reasons for running away.'

The insinuation in his voice sends my heart and legs fleeing. I run away into the darkness of the driveway with the sound of their laughter hitting my back.

'What's your problem?' my brother asks as I slam the car door and buckle my seatbelt, panting and fixing my short strands of hair back into place. 'Why were you running?'

'Mom said to hurry.' I fix my eyes on my lap.

'I sometimes wonder about you, Callie.' He rearranges his dark brown hair into place and slumps back in the seat. 'It's like you go out of your way to make people think you're a freak.'

'I'm not a twenty-four-year-old who's hanging around at a high-school party,' I remind him.

My mom narrows her eyes at me. 'Callie, don't start. You know Mr. Owens invited your brother, just like he invited you to the party.'

My mind drifts back to Kayden, his face beaten and bruised. I feel horrible for leaving him and almost tell my mom what happened, but then I catch a glimpse of Caleb and Daisy on the front porch, watching us back away, and I remember that sometimes secrets need to be taken to the grave. Besides, my mom has never been one for wanting to hear about the ugly things in the world.

'I'm only twenty-three. I don't turn twenty-four until next month,' my brother interrupts my thoughts. 'And they're not in high school anymore, so shut your mouth.'

'I know how old you are,' I say. 'And I'm not in high school either.'

306

'You don't need to sound so happy about it,' my mom grimaces as she spins the steering wheel to pull out onto the street. Wrinkles crease around her hazel eyes as she tries not to cry. 'We're going to miss you and I really wish you'd reconsider waiting until fall to go away to school. Laramie is almost six hours away, sweetie. It's going to be so hard being that far away from you.'

I stare at the road that stretches through the trees and over the shallow hills. 'Sorry, Mom, but I'm already enrolled. Besides, there's no point in me sticking around for the summer just to sit around in my room.'

'You could always get a job,' she suggests. 'Like your brother does every summer. That way you can spend some time with him, and Caleb is going to be staying with us.'

Every muscle in my body winds up like a knotted rope and I have to force oxygen into my lungs. 'Sorry, Mom, but I'm ready to be on my own.'

I'm more than ready. I'm sick of the sad looks she always gives me because she doesn't understand anything I do. I'm tired of wanting to tell her what happened, but knowing I can't. I'm ready to be on my own, away from the nightmares that haunt my room, my life, my whole world.

Chapter One

#4: Wear a Shirt with Color.

4 months later...

Callie

I often wonder what drives people to do things. Whether it's put into their minds at birth, or if it is learned as they grow. Maybe it's even forced upon them by circumstances that are out of their hands. Does anyone have control over their lives or are we all helpless?

'God, it's like spazzville around here today,' Seth comments, scrunching his nose at the arriving freshmen swarming the campus yard. Then he waves his hand in front of my face. 'Are you spacing off on me again?'

I blink away from my thoughts. 'Now don't be arrogant.' I nudge his shoulder with mine playfully. 'Just

308

because we both decided to do the summer semester and we know where everything is doesn't make us better than them.'

'Uh, yeah, it kind of does.' He rolls his honey-brown eyes at me. 'We're like the upper-class freshmen.'

I press back a smile and sip my latte. 'You know there's no such thing as an upper-class freshman.'

He sighs, ruffling his golden-blond locks, which look like he gets them highlighted in a salon, but they're actually natural. 'Yeah, I know. Especially for people like you and me. We're like two black sheep.'

'There are many more black sheep than you and me.' I shield my eyes from the sun with my hand. 'And I've toned it down. I'm even wearing a red T-shirt today, like the list said to do.'

The corners of his lips tug upward. 'Which would look even better if you'd let those pretty locks of yours down, instead of hiding them in that ponytail all the time.'

'One step at a time,' I say. 'It was hard enough just letting my hair grow out. It makes me feel weird. And it doesn't matter because that has yet to be added to the list.'

'Well it needs to be,' he replies. 'In fact, I'm doing it when I get back to my room.'

Seth and I have a list of things we have to do, even if we're scared, repulsed, or incapable. If it's on the list, we have to do it and we have to cross off one thing at least once a week. It was something we did after we confessed our darkest secrets to each other, locked away in my room, during my first real bonding moment with a human being.

'And you still wear that God-awful hoodie,' he continues, jerking on the bottom of my gray faded jacket. 'I thought we talked about that hideous thing. You're beautiful and you don't need to cover up. Besides, it's like eighty degrees outside.'

I wrap my jacket around myself self-consciously, gripping at the edge of the fabric. 'Subject change, please.'

He loops arms with mine as he leans his weight on me, forcing me to scoot over to the edge of the sidewalk as people pass by us. 'Fine, but one day we're going to talk about a complete makeover, in which I will supervise.'

I sigh. 'We'll see.'

I met Seth my first day at UW during Pre-Calculus. Our inability to understand numbers was a great conversation starter and our friendship kind of grew from there. Seth is the only friend I've really had since sixth grade, besides a brief friendship with the new girl in school who didn't know the 'Anorexic, Devil-Worshipping Callie' everyone else saw me as.

Seth abruptly stops walking and swings in front of me. He's wearing a gray T-shirt and a pair of black skinny jeans. His hair is stylishly tousled and his long eyelashes are the envy of every girl.

'I just have to say one more thing.' He touches the tip of his finger to the corner of my eye. 'I like the maroon eyeliner much better than the excessive black.'

'I have your approval on that.' I press my hand dramatically to my heart. 'I'm so relieved. It's been weighing on my mind since this morning.'

He makes a face and his eyes scroll down my red T-shirt that brushes the top of my form-fitting jeans. 'You're doing great in every department, I just wish you'd wear a dress or shorts or something for once and show off those legs of yours.'

My face plummets along with my mood. 'Seth, you know why...I mean, you know...I can't...'

'I know. I'm just trying to be encouraging.'

'I know you are and that's why I love you.' I love him for more than that, actually. I love him because he's the first person I felt comfortable enough with to tell my secrets to, but maybe that's because he understands what it's like to be hurt inside and out.

'You're so much happier than when I first met you.' He tucks my bangs behind my ear. 'I wish you could be this way around everyone, Callie. That you would stop hiding from everyone. It's sad no one gets to see how great you are.'

'And vice versa,' I say, because Seth hides as much as I do.

He takes my empty Styrofoam cup from my hand and tosses it into a garbage can beside one of the benches. 'What do you think? Should we hit up one of the tours and make fun of the tour guide?'

'You know the way to my heart.' I beam and his laughter lights up his entire face.

We stroll up the sidewalk in the shade of the trees toward the front doors of the main office, which is a few stories high with a peaked roof. It has a historical look to it, tan brick with a lot of wear and tear, like it belongs in an older era. The yard that centers all the buildings looks like a triangular maze with randomly placed concrete paths that cross the lawn. It's a pretty place to go to school, lots of trees, and open space, but it took some getting used to.

There is confusion in the air as students and parents attempt to find their way around. I'm completely distracted when I hear a faint, 'Heads up.'

312

My head snaps up just in time to see a guy running straight for me with his hands in the air and a football flying at him. His solid body collides with mine and I fall flat onto my back, cracking my head and elbow against the pavement. Pain erupts through my arm and I can't breathe.

'Get off me,' I say, writhing my body in a panic. The weight and heat off him makes me feel like I'm drowning. 'Get off now!'

'I'm so sorry.' He rolls to the side and quickly climbs off me. 'I didn't see you there.'

I blink the spots away from my eyes until his face comes into focus; brown hair that flips up at the ears, piercing emerald eyes, and a smile that will melt a girl's heart. 'Kayden?'

His eyebrows furrow and his hand falls to his side. 'Do I know you?' There's a small scar below his right eye and I wonder if it's from where his dad hit him that night.

A tiny prickle forms in my heart that he can't remember who I am. Getting to my feet, I brush the dirt and grass off my sleeves. 'Um, no, sorry. I thought you were someone else.'

'But you got the name right.' His tone carries doubt as he scoops the football off the grass. 'Wait, I do know you, don't I?'

'I'm really sorry for getting in your way.' I snag Seth's hand and haul him toward the entrance doors where there's a big 'Welcome Students' banner.

When we're in the corridor by the glass display cases, I let go of him and lean against the brick wall, catching my breath. 'That was Kayden Owens.'

'*Oh.*' He glances back at the entrance as students swarm inside. '*The* Kayden Owens? The one you saved?'

'I didn't save him,' I clarify. 'I just interrupted something.'

'Something that was about to get ugly.'

'Anyone would have done the same thing.'

His fingers seize my elbow as I attempt to walk down the hall and he pulls me back to him. 'No, a lot of people would have walked by. It's a common fact that a lot of people will turn their heads in the other direction when something bad is happening. I know this from experience.'

My heart aches for him and what he went through. 'I'm sorry you had to go through that.'

'Don't be sorry, Callie,' he says with a heavy-hearted sigh. 'You have your own sad story.'

We make our way down the slender hallway until it opens up and there is a table stacked with flyers and pamphlets on it. People are standing in line, staring at schedules, talking to their parents, looking scared and excited.

'He didn't even recognize you,' he comments as he works through the crowd to the front of the line, cutting in front of everyone, and grabs a pink flyer.

'He barely recognized me ever,' I shake my head when he offers me a cookie from a plate on the table.

'Well, he should recognize you now.' He picks up a sugar cookie, scrapes the sprinkles off, and bites off the corner. Crumbs fall from his lips as he chews. 'You did save his ass from getting beat.'

'It's not that big of a deal,' I say, even though it does stab at my heart a little. 'Now, can we please change the subject to something else?'

'It is a big deal.' He sighs when I frown at him. 'Fine, I'll keep my mouth shut. Now come on, let's go find a tour guide to torture.'

Kayden

I've been haunted by a nightmare every single God damn night for the last four months. I'm curled up near the pool house and my dad's beating the shit out of me. He's madder than I've ever seen him, probably because I did one of the worst things imaginable to him. There's murder in his eyes and every ounce of humanity is gone, consumed by rage.

As his fist hammers against my face, warm blood pours along my skin and splatters against his shirt. I know this time he's probably going to kill me and I should finally fight back, but I was taught to die on the inside. Plus I just don't seem to care anymore.

Then someone appears from the shadows and interrupts us. When I wipe the blood from my eyes, I realize it's a girl terrified out of her mind. I don't quite understand it, why she intervened, but I owe her a lot.

Callie Lawrence saved my fucking life that night, more than she probably realized. I wish she knew, but I never could figure out how to tell her, nor have I seen her since it happened. I heard she went off to college early to start her life and I envy her.

My first day on campus is going pretty well, especially after my mom and dad left. Once they drove away, I could breathe for the very first time in my life.

Luke and I wander around the busy campus trying to figure out where everything is, while tossing a football back and forth. The sun is bright, the trees are green, and there's so much newness in the air it gets me pumped up. I want to start over, be happy, live for once.

On a particularly long throw, I end up running over a girl. I feel like an asshole, especially because she's so small and fragile-looking. Her blue eyes are enlarged and she looks scared to death. What's even weirder is she knows me, but takes off running when I question how she does.

It's bugging the hell out of me. I can't stop thinking about her face and the familiarity. Why can't I figure out who the hell she is?

'Did you see that girl?' I ask Luke. He's been my best friend since second grade when we both realized how mutually screwed up our home lives were, although for different reasons.

'The one you just ran over?' He folds up the schedule and tucks it into his back pocket of his jeans. 'She kind of reminds me of that quiet girl we used to go to school with—the one Daisy was dead set on torturing.'

My eyes move to the entrance doors where she disappeared. 'Callie Lawrence?'

'Yeah, I think that was her name.' He blows out a stressed breath as he turns around in the middle of the lawn, trying to get his bearings. 'But I don't think it's her. She wasn't wearing all that black shit around her eyes and Callie had a haircut that made her look like a guy. Plus, I think that girl was thinner.'

'Yeah, she did look different.' But if it is Callie, I need to talk to her about that night. 'Callie was always thin, though. That's why Daisy made fun of her.'

'That was one of the reasons she made fun of her,' he reminds me and his face twists with repulsion at something behind me. 'I think I'm going to go find our room.' Luke hurries off toward the corner of the school building before I can say anything.

'There you are.' Daisy comes up from behind me and I'm overwhelmed by the smell of perfume and hairspray.

Suddenly I understand why Luke ran off like there was a fire. He doesn't like Daisy for many reasons; one being that he thinks Daisy is a bitch. And she is, but it works for me because she allows me to stay detached from feeling anything, which is the only way I know how to live life.

'I sure hope you weren't just talking about me.' Daisy wraps her arms around my midsection and massages my stomach with her fingertips. 'Unless it was something good.'

I turn around and kiss her forehead. She's wearing a low-cut blue dress and a necklace that rests between her tits. 'No one was talking about you. Luke just went to find his room.'

She bites down on her glossy lip and bats her eyelashes at me. 'Good, because I'm already nervous about leaving my ridiculously hot boyfriend. Remember you can flirt, but you can't touch.' Daisy gets bored easily and says things to start drama.

'No touching. Got it,' I say, holding back an eye roll. 'And again, no one was talking about you.'

She twines a strand of her curly blonde hair around her finger with a thoughtful expression on her face. 'I don't mind if you talk about me, just as long as it's good.'

I met Daisy when I was in tenth grade and she moved to our school. She was the hot new freshman and was very aware that she was. I was pretty popular, but hadn't really dated anyone, just messed around. I was more focused on football, like my dad wanted me to be. Daisy seemed interested, though, and a couple of weeks later, we were officially a couple. She's self-involved and she never asks where all my bruises, cuts, and scars come from. She brought it up once, the first time we fucked, and I told her it was from a four-wheeling accident when I was a kid. She didn't question the fresh ones.

'Look, baby, I got to go.' I give her a quick kiss on the lips. 'I have to check in and unpack and figure out where the hell everything is.'

'Oh, fine.' She pouts out her bottom lip and runs her fingers through my hair, guiding my lips back to hers for a deep kiss. When she pulls away, she smiles. 'I guess I'll go back home and try to fill up my time with boring old high school.'

'I'm sure you'll be fine,' I say to her as I back toward the doors, maneuvering between the people flooding the sidewalk. 'I'll be back for homecoming.'

She waves as she turns for the parking lot. I keep my eyes on her until she's in her car and then I go into the school. The air is cooler inside, the lights are faint, and there's a lot of shouting and disorganization.

'We don't need a tour.' I walk up to Luke, who's standing near the sign-up table, reading a pink flyer. 'And weren't you going to find your room, or was that your excuse to escape Daisy?'

'The girl drives me fucking crazy.' He rakes his hand

through his short brown hair. 'And I was headed there, but then I realized it'd be much easier if I went on a tour so I know where everything is.'

Luke is a very structured person when it comes to school and sports. It makes sense to me since I know about his past, but from an outsider's point of view he probably looks like a troublemaker who failed out of school.

'Fine, we'll do the tour.' I write our names down on the paper and the redhead sitting behind the table smiles at me.

'You can go join the one starting now,' she says shamelessly pushing her cleavage up with her arms as she leans forward. 'They just stepped into the hallway.'

'Thanks.' Grinning at her, I strut off with Luke toward where she directed us.

'Every time,' he says amusedly as he sidesteps around a smaller table with plates full of cookies on it. 'You're like a magnet.'

'I don't ask for it,' I reply as we approach the back of the crowd. 'In fact, I wish they'd stop.'

'No you don't,' he states with a roll of his eyes. 'You love it and you know it. And I wished you'd act on it, so you could ditch the bitch.'

'Daisy's not that bad. She's probably the only girl

who doesn't care if I flirt.' I cross my arms and stare at the nerdy tour guide with thick glasses, scraggily brown hair, and a clipboard in his hands. 'Do we really need to do this? I'd rather go unpack.'

'I need to know where everything is,' he says. 'You can go to the room if you want.'

'I'm fine here.' My eyes zone in on a girl across the crowd; the one I ran over. She's smiling at a guy next to her who's whispering something in her ear. I find myself entertained by the naturalness of it, no pretenses like the ones I'm used to seeing.

'What are you looking at?' Luke tracks my gaze and his forehead creases. 'You know what? I think that might be Callie Lawrence. Now that I think about it, I remember her dad mentioning something about her going to UW.'

'No way...it can't be...is it?' I take in her brown hair, her clothes that show her thin frame, and her blue eyes that sparkle as she laughs. The last time I saw her, those blue eyes were clouded and weighted. The Callie I knew held more darkness, wore baggy clothes, and always looked sad. She shied away from everyone, except for that one night when she saved my ass.

'No, it's her,' Luke says with confidence as he flicks

his finger against his temple. 'Remember she had that small birthmark on her temple just like that girl does. It can't be a freakish coincidence.'

'Fuck me,' I say loudly and everyone looks at me.

'Can I help you?' the tour guide asks in an icy tone.

I shake my head, noticing Callie is staring at me. 'Sorry man, I thought a bee landed on me.'

Luke snorts a laugh and I suppress my laughter. The tour guide huffs in frustration and continues his speech about where all the offices are as he points at each door.

'What was that about?' Luke asks in a low voice as he folds a paper neatly in half.

'Nothing.' I skim the crowd, but Callie's nowhere. 'Did you see where she went?'

Luke shakes his head. 'Nope.'

My eyes travel across the hallway, but there's no sign of her anywhere. I need to find her, so I can thank her for saving my life, like I should have done four months ago.

Don't miss Jessica's latest, passionate series.

Begin with the first book,

Breaking Nova

Nova Reed used to have dreams of becoming a famous drummer, of marrying her true love. But all of that was taken away in an instant. Now she's getting by as best she can, though sometimes that means doing things the old Nova would never do. Things that are slowly eating away at her spirit. Every day blends into the next, until she meets Quinton Carter.

Quinton once got a second chance at life, but he doesn't want it. The tattoos on his chest are a constant reminder of what he's done, what he's lost. He's sworn to never allow happiness into his life, but then beautiful, sweet Nova makes him smile. He knows he's too damaged to get close to her, yet she's the only one who can make him feel alive again. Quinton will have to decide: does he deserve to start over? Or should he pay for his past forever?

Out now.